S

BY

REBECCA LANG

MILLS & BOON®

First published in Great Britain 1998
Harlequin Mills & Boon Limited,
Eton House, 18-24 Paradise Road, Richmond, Surrey TW9 1SR

ISBN 0 263 80640 5

Set in Times 10 on 11½ pt. by
Rowland Phototypesetting Limited
Bury St Edmunds, Suffolk

03-9802-51965-D

Printed and bound in Great Britain
by Mackays of Chatham PLC, Chatham

CHAPTER ONE

'EXCUSE me, are you a doctor?'

The man turned, his hand on the latch of the car door, a look of guarded surprise on his face.

'Please, are you a doctor?' the young woman repeated. 'I need help. I'm going to have a baby.'

There was desperation in her voice, making the man pause in his act of unlocking the car that was parked on the ground level of the hospital multi-storey parking lot.

Statistically, he found himself thinking, something like this was bound to happen sooner or later. He straightened up and took in the woman's appearance.

Her face was very pale, distraught, her hair somewhat dishevelled. Understandable. His eyes travelled over her obviously pregnant body which was wrapped in an enveloping thick coat. She clutched the coat to her with gloveless hands that were tight with tension, as well as mottled with cold. Also, she had very obviously been crying.

As his eyes travelled downwards, over her legs which were clothed in sheer, thin stockings—inadequate against the cold of an early December evening in Ontario—down over her shoes, he saw the pool of fluid that had gathered at her feet. Then, as he watched, a thin stream of blood moved slowly down her pale leg and settled in an irregular-shaped blot on the instep of her foot.

Galvanized into action, he reached for her arm. 'Yes, I am a doctor,' he said tersely. 'Come with me.'

As he led her quickly around the back of his car, aware that at any moment she might collapse, he heard her indrawn breath and sensed her pain. A wave of compassion came over him. It came as a relief—sometimes these days he thought he had lost it for ever.

When the door was open he leaned into the car, pressing down the lever that lowered the soft leather back of the passenger seat so that it was almost flat, forming a couch. Women in the last stage of pregnancy shouldn't be out alone, he thought, his irritation not directed at the waif-faced woman but at the absent man who had fathered her child. Where the hell was her husband? He ought to be with her, particularly on a night like this.

By the look of the voluminous cashmere coat she was wearing, the good leather shoes and the smart handbag that she carried, she was not from the ranks of the poor women, some of them homeless, who came into hospital emergency departments in the city's downtown core when they were in labour, having had no antenatal care whatsoever.

No, she was not one of those, he considered. Yet she had something about her. . .that same look, the same aura of aloneness. Yes, she was frightened, like they were under the bravado that they commonly displayed. She did not have that bravado, although her vulnerability was evident. Instead, there was something else about her, an underlying quiet, calm strength.

'Sit there,' he instructed her, standing back and opening the car door wide. 'Sit there, then lie back. You'll feel better with your head down. I'll get you to University Hospital Emergency Department. That's the best thing, I think. Are you from Gresham?'

'Yes. . . I know the hospital.'

'Good. Take it easy,' he said. He tried to make his voice gentle, reassuring, aware of the risk he was taking with this unknown woman—a risk something like the one he had taken before, with disastrous results. Once was enough—more than enough. To say that the experience had ruined his life was only a slight exaggeration.

'Thank you. I'm very grateful.' Her voice was soft, well modulated, the fear coming through. 'The. . .the baby isn't actually due for another three weeks. I thought I would be all right coming out. I. . .was just sitting in my car, over there. . .'

As she bent to get into the car, ungainly, awkward, he leaned forward to help her, gripping her arm firmly. That protective gentleness that he felt was the very thing that had got him into trouble. Yet he wouldn't be much of a doctor without it. There were too many doctors who acted like automatons, couldn't deal with the stress of their emotions or denied them altogether. Such individuals ought to be in laboratories torturing rats, he had always thought, doing so-called research. . .

Just be careful, the inner voice warned. Don't flatter yourself with this woman, but just be careful. 'You're bleeding,' he said, his voice more brusque than he had intended. 'How long has that been going on?'

'Not long,' she said quietly as she settled herself into the comfortable seat and lay back. 'Just a few moments. I was in my car, driving along, when the membranes ruptured. So I drove in here. I used to work here, you see. . . at University Hospital.'

'Before the membranes ruptured, did you have pain?'

'Yes. . .a little. For a while.'

'In what capacity did you work there?' he asked, tucking her coat around her legs quickly and glancing at her abnormally pale face as she lay back and closed her eyes.

'I'm a nurse,' she said faintly.

'How long since the membranes ruptured?' he asked urgently.

'About fifteen minutes, I think. I didn't notice any blood at first. My. . .my blood pressure's been up a bit lately.

But I think that was due to. . .emotional factors. At least, I thought so at the time. . .' Her voice trailed away on a gasp of pain.

'Are you having contractions?'

'Yes.'

He slammed the car door, walked quickly round to the driver's side and got in beside her. Adjusting his seat belt, he looked sideways at her face. It had been a while since he had delivered a baby, but it was an art which once learned was never forgotten. Better get her to the emergency department as quickly as possible. He started the engine and put the car into reverse.

She should not be bleeding, not this bright red blood, so early in labour. Not in a normal labour. Maybe she had a placenta praevia, the placenta too low down in the uterus so that it partly covered the cervix and then started to bleed as the cervix dilated at the start of labour. If it continued the baby could be stillborn, deprived of oxygen.

On the other hand, it could be a placenta abruptio, a premature separation of the placenta, he thought, going over in his mind with lightning speed all the possibilities of an inappropriate ante-partum haemorrhage. After all, she had mentioned high blood pressure. . .

'Maybe I should have gone to the emergency department myself,' the woman said apologetically, 'but I just wanted to get off the street quickly. I. . .thought I might faint, you see, at the wheel.'

'Yes,' he said. 'You did the right thing. There are lots of doctors passing through here, I imagine. We'll be there in a few minutes. Hang in there!'

The powerful car made scarcely a sound as he eased it in line behind two other cars at the check-out point, where he would show his visiting MD pass and drive out without having to waste time in paying.

'I'm so grateful.' the woman whispered again. 'I don't

want to lose this baby. I think I'd go mad if I lost it.'

When he glanced at her she still had her eyes closed. She might have been talking to herself.

'My name's Stanton. . . Lisa Stanton,' she said, looking at him. 'I'm actually booked to have the baby at the Raeburn Clinic, not University Hospital, so they won't have any of my records here.'

'Can't be helped,' he said, showing his temporary pass at the check-out and driving smoothly out to the street where the tarmac was slick with rainwater. It glistened in the glow of streetlamps which were just coming on in the early dusk. 'I don't think you have time to get to the Raeburn Clinic.'

'No. . .' she agreed ruefully, a wealth of meaning in that one word. He even heard a tinge of humour and admired her for it.

University Hospital, Gresham, filled a whole city block, a conglomerate of buildings, some quite old and some very recent. The emergency department was only a few hundred yards from where they were now, on a street at right angles to where they were. They just had to drive to the intersection and make a right turn. Sometimes that intersection could be busy, he reflected, now that the rush hour was on—which made him realize that he had nothing much to go home for, except to relax.

'I'm Marcus Blair,' he said, as the car accelerated smoothly into the stream of traffic on the side-street. For a moment he took his eyes off the road to look at her, and saw her watching him. It was then he noticed, by the light of the streetlamps, that her eyes were blue, a beautiful clear blue that contrasted so well with her pale skin and thick auburn hair.

'You work at University Hospital, Dr Blair?' she asked.

'No, not yet. I'm planning to in the very near future. I was just visiting.'

At the traffic lights he made a quick right turn. In a matter of seconds they were pulling into the short semi-circular driveway in front of the main entrance to the emergency department, under cover of the concrete roof awning. An ambulance was parked ahead of them.

'Don't move yet,' he said, 'I'll get a stretcher organized.'

'Thank you. . .' Lisa Stanton watched his tall figure striding away from her through the automatic double doors. Thank God she had met him, that he had come along just when she so desperately needed someone. If he hadn't come she would have had to pull out again into the stream of traffic or ask the attendant at the parking garage to call her an ambulance.

She felt safe with this man, Dr Marcus Blair. Presumably he wasn't an obstetrician—he would have said. As she closed her eyes against the harsh glare of the fluorescent lights another contraction started in her uterus and she tried to relax, to go with it, as she waited. Very deliberately, since she had first noticed the blood, she had tried not to think about the possible causes of the bleeding, even though she understood the implications only too well. To prevent an upsurge of panic she had concentrated instead on trying not to faint when light-headedness had come over her as she had looked around desperately for help.

Now she found that it helped to keep Dr Blair's image in her mind—to concentrate on his face, with its dark, penetrating eyes, the firm, decisive features, the crisp, dark hair, cut short. . .

He seemed so dependable, not like Rich— Oh, damn! She had vowed not to say his name, not even to herself, while she was giving birth, not even to think about him if she could possibly help it. Because if she thought of him she would expect something of him, would be tempted to get in touch with him somehow—and that would only confirm what she already knew. It was all over with him; there would be nothing forthcoming from that direction. It didn't matter—she could manage quite well without him. This way, maybe she could think of the baby as all hers.

Steeling herself against another, sharper pain and willing herself not to tense her muscles, she realized that it would be impossible not to let thoughts of Richard sneak into her consciousness. After all, it was normal for the father of a baby to be there when that baby was born. Or was she living in some sort of dream world that she applied to herself when many other women in the real world, she knew from experience, often had something different?

There was a flurry of activity and voices. The car door was flung open. 'You don't have to do anything,' Dr Blair instructed her. 'We're going to lift you out onto the stretcher.' There were four other people with him—two were porters.

Vaguely, Lisa was aware that she was bleeding again as they lifted her onto the stretcher. All at once she felt faint and slightly nauseated. The stretcher began to move in under the bright lights as the emergency department staff continued to pile blankets on her. She lay flat, with no pillow, so that as she was moved along the ceiling was all that she could see, with its lights like bright, staring eyes. They added to her sudden sense of disorientation.

'Dr Blair?' she said, surprised at the smallness of her own voice.

'I'm still here,' he said, coming into her line of vision as he bent over her, walking beside the stretcher. 'Almost there. I've got the senior obstetrics resident lined up to see you, and there's a staff obstetrician on his way, apparently.'

'Would you stay with me. . .please?'

The stretcher made a sharp turn, then they were in an examination room behind curtains. Lisa found herself being lifted onto a different kind of stretcher. There seemed to be doctors and nurses everywhere.

She put up a hand to Dr Blair who stood beside her, overcome with a fear that she would be left alone. In the few minutes that she had known him he seemed to represent normality, a sane compass point in a world that was becoming unpredictable. An irrational fear was coming over her that if she lost sight of him she would somehow sink down into a vortex of spiralling circumstances over which she had no control. . .

'Sure,' he said, his warm brown eyes locking with hers for a second. 'I'm going to be right here.'

As he took her hand Lisa realized that his face was becoming increasingly blurred and that the lights set in the ceiling were curiously fuzzy. At the same time she felt cold—very, very cold. There was no mistaking what it meant. She was bleeding seriously.

'Richard. . .?' She murmured the name as she clung to the warm hand. With all her failing strength she squeezed that hand. 'Stay with me.'

Figures moved in and out of her line of vision—blurred, white-coated figures, nurses in pale pink and blue jumpsuits. A plastic mask was fitted over her nose and mouth and a strap around her head. 'Breathe in some oxygen, Mrs Stanton. Just breathe normally.'

'Get up an IV, quick. Make it dextrose-saline,' a voice said, surprisingly loud, and Lisa felt the sting of an IV cannula going into the back of her left hand. At the same time she was aware that her clothes were being taken off and the cool pad of a stethoscope was being placed on her abdomen.

'Blood pressure cuff on. BP's a bit low,' someone said.

'Foetal heart rate slightly elevated. Circulating oxygen level OK. Fair amount of vaginal bleeding.'

'Thank God,' Lisa murmured, feeling tears of relief seep from the corners of her closed eyelids. 'Don't let anything happen to my baby. . .please.'

'We won't.' It was the voice of Dr Blair. 'Take it easy.'

'Got those blood samples?' a terse voice asked, rising above the bustle of activity around the stretcher.

'Yeah. . .just about.'

'I want a haemoglobin done on that blood—prothrombin-time and clotting-time. Stat. OK? Make sure the stat lab knows it's coming. And get them to do a cross-match right away. In the meantime, get me a couple of packs of the O negative. Hang them up. Stat! I want plasma too—get that up. I want to put in a second IV. Get on to the operating room.'

'We're doing that right now!'

'Get that foetal monitor going.'

'It's on.'

'I want a Foley catheter put in—continuous drainage.'

The tense male voice that had been issuing instructions addressed Lisa. 'Mrs Stanton, I'm Dr Rick Kates, the senior obstetrics resident. Who's your obstetrician at the Raeburn Clinic? Your husband told me you were booked in there.' He lifted up the plastic face mask so that she could speak.

Lisa opened her eyes, knowing that she was in serious trouble when she could not focus properly on his face. A nurse was hanging up a pack of blood.

'Dr Charles Linton.' The words came out through dry, stiff lips.

'OK, we'll contact him.' The resident bent down close to her. 'Can you tell us your due date, and whether you had an ultrasound done during the pregnancy?'

'I'm due at the end of December, the thirty-first,' she

said, fighting to control the awful fear in her as she felt gushes of warm blood flowing from her body. 'Yes, I had two ultarasounds—the last one was about three weeks ago.'

'Did Dr Linton say anything to you about a placenta praevia, Mrs Stanton?'

'No. . .no, he didn't.'

'You're a nurse, I understand?'

'Yes.'

'You're aware that you're bleeding?' She nodded. 'We don't know why yet, but it looks as though the placenta is separating prematurely. When did you last have anything to eat or drink?'

'Not since. . .' She calculated slowly, her mind sluggish. 'Not since midday—a glass of milk, a few crackers.'

'Right! That's good, even though it means your blood sugar's probably low. We're going to have to do a Caesarean section, Mrs Stanton. We have to get that baby out. We're waiting for the staff man to get here. So far, the foetal heart rate's OK. You're doing all right.'

As the resident moved away from the side of the stretcher a nurse, holding another plastic bag of blood, took his place. 'Excuse me, Mr Stanton,' the nurse said, looking at Dr Blair, 'I just want to get in here to hang up the blood. Then we have to put in a urinary catheter, then another IV.'

'OK,' Marcus Blair said. 'I'll make myself as inconspicuous as possible, although I know my wife would appreciate me being able to hold her hand.'

Realizing that the staff had taken Marcus Blair to be her husband, and that he had obviously not corrected the assumption, her eyes sought his in mute apology. She hadn't intended him to be involved in such a way—it had just happened. There was something about him that invited trust. Many other men would have just taken off as soon as the hospital staff had taken over. There was no denying that she needed him, or someone just like him, at this moment.

As his eyes met hers Lisa acknowledged the ironic gleam in them, the slight raising of his eyebrows as he accepted the duplicity. His mouth quirked in a slight smile at the shared secret.

In moments more blood from the IV was dripping into a secondary tubing that ran into a vein. Everything was moving fast—events were out of her control, as though they had taken on a momentum of their own. In very short order, a urinary catheter had been inserted in her bladder.

'Lisa.' Marcus Blair was bending close to her, his voice barely audible. 'Is there anyone I can contact for you? Your husband? The nurses will want to know your next of kin. They'll have to know it's not me.'

'I haven't got a husband,' she said quietly, her eyes meeting his candidly. 'I'd appreciate it if you'd let my mother know. . .later, after the baby's born. I don't want her to know now. . .it's too late for her to get here. . . she'll worry too much. The number's in my bag, in my address book. Take my bag—here.' She handed it over. 'Keep it with you, please.'

'Sure. No one else?' he persisted.

'No.'

'What about Richard?' he said gently, in an undertone.

'What do you know about Richard?'

'You said the name more than once. Is he the father?'

He did not equivocate, and Lisa found that she was relieved. With her free hand she smoothed back damp tendrils of hair from her clammy forehead, trying to gather her thoughts into some sort of coherence. It was so much easier to talk to a stranger, anyway. After this she might never see him again, although with a piercing, poignant longing she wished that she might. . .

'Lisa?'

'I. . . Yes, he is the father. But I don't want him contacted.'

The nurse interrupted again. 'Will you take her personal belongings, Mr Stanton? Her bag, and so on?' In her hands was a large, clear plastic bag, the type used for garbage, through which Lisa recognized her blood-stained coat and her shoes.

Surprisingly she felt no embarrassment that a stranger was claiming her personal belongings as the nurse handed them over to him. She was beyond embarrassment. Indeed, she felt oddly distanced from it, as though it were happening to someone else, even though everything was registering with unusual clarity. Perhaps that was what extreme fear did to you—fear that she would lose her baby, perhaps her own life.

For months now she had loved that baby growing inside her with a fierce, intense love that she had not previously thought possible. With each week of the pregnancy that love had increased, together with a powerful, protective urge, so that she felt she would go through fire for the safety of that child—in spite of Richard.

Then there was a renewed flurry of activity as the staff obstetrician arrived, and Lisa was behind closed curtains so that she could be examined and asked more questions. Marcus Blair had stepped away from her.

At the end of it the obstetrician, a grey-haired, middle-aged man with a kindly face, patted her consolingly on the shoulder.

'I want to take you to the operating room, do a Caesarean section,' he said. 'So far, everything's OK, but it won't be OK very soon if we wait. I'm sorry, but there's no alternative. Sometimes these things happen, with no immediately obvious explanation.'

'I'm quite prepared for that,' Lisa said calmly, as she

held the precious oxygen mask a few inches away from her face. 'I don't want anything to happen to this baby... don't want to take any risks.'

'That's my girl!' he said encouragingly, not intending to be paternalistic or patronizing, 'We'll have that baby out in no time. I'll see you again in a few minutes in the operating room. And, don't you worry, everything's under control.' With another squeeze of her shoulder he was gone, his small entourage with him.

'Show me those blood-work results as soon as you get them,' Lisa heard his voice demanding from a distance. 'And get the other units of blood right away. Get that plasma hooked up.'

Only then did Lisa feel her composure slip, feel a tightening of her throat—a moment of sheer panic.

'Marcus?' The nurses thought he was her husband so she could hardly call him Dr Blair.

'I'm here, Lisa.' Then he was beside her again, had become reassuringly familiar. Again he took her hand, covering its coldness with both his own.

'They're taking me to the operating room now,' she whispered. 'I wanted to say thank you again. You've been so kind. I've taken up so much of your time.'

'Would you say goodbye to her now, Mr Stanton?' A nurse hurried in behind the privacy curtains. 'We're taking her to the OR right away.'

'Sure,' Marcus Blair said. 'Give me a moment.' For the nurse's benefit, no doubt, Lisa thought, he kissed her on the cheek and put his arms around her for a few brief seconds, the gesture bringing a lump of emotion to her throat. Automatically she kissed him back, allowing herself to give way to the relief of the brief welcome closeness.

'I'll be there in the recovery room when you come round from the anaesthetic—let you know whether you've had a girl or a boy,' he said softly, his cheek against hers, this stranger whom she had met fortuitously in a parking lot. It should have been Richard. How strange were the outcomes of dire need, she thought desperately, reluctant to let him go.

'How?' she whispered back.

'I'll find a way,' he said. He let her go then, pushing her back onto the stretcher and pulling the cotton blanket up over her shoulders to keep her warm. 'Good luck, and don't worry. Look at that. . .' He indicated the foetal monitor at the bedside, where the spiky heartbeats of her unborn child showed up clearly on the screen. 'That baby's holding its own, in spite of everything.'

'Yes. . .' She smiled.

'Are you sure you don't want me to contact Richard?' he persisted gently.

'Yes, I'm sure,' she said. 'You see. . .he doesn't know I'm pregnant.'

'Here we go, Mrs Stanton.' The nurse was back, brushing aside the curtains briskly with a no-nonsense finality, 'The porter's here now to take you to the OR.' She efficiently released the brakes on the stretcher. 'Won't be long now. You'll soon be holding that lovely baby in your arms.'

The stretcher began to move, a porter at one end and the nurse at the other.

'See you soon.' Dr Blair, playing the part of the loving husband, without which he might have been politely asked to leave long ago, kissed her cheek again, as though in silent response to her imploring eyes. Then the warm hand released hers for the last time.

'Thanks,' she whispered. 'Goodbye. . .Marcus.'

The porter set a brisk pace, propelling the stretcher from corridor to elevator to corridor again and then at last to the wide automatic doors of the operating suite. Lisa knew those doors so well from her professional life, a life that seemed a million years away.

With her free hand she felt her swollen abdomen under cover of the enveloping blankets. Then she felt the baby move inside her, the slow, familiar slight changing of position—the stretching of the limbs, the sudden kick of a foot—that it made every so often. Then her eyes filled with tears, tears of relief. 'We'll make it,' she said fiercely to herself. 'We'll both make it.'

Her tears were of gratitude as well to a strange man who fully understood what being a doctor really meant. The memory of his kiss would stay with her like a talisman while she waited for the anaesthetic, even though it was Richard's child she carried, Richard she loved. . .

Then the stretcher came to a halt in a quiet area.

'Lisa! Lisa Stanton! Isn't it?' a voice said.

A nurse bent over Lisa when she opened her eyes. They were in a small anteroom beside the main obstetrics operating room in the vast operating suite.

'Yes, it is,' she agreed weakly, lifting the oxygen mask so that she could answer. 'Leonora! Is it really you?' The woman bending over her had been a colleague.

'It's me, all right.' The nurse smiled.

'Thank God for a familiar face,' Lisa sighed. 'I. . .don't know the staff man or the resident.'

'Both new,' the nurse said briskly, pressing Lisa's hand. 'And both superb at their jobs, I might add. . .in case you doubted it. But you know that you get the best at University Hospital, don't you?'

'Sure.' Lisa smiled back. 'It's so great to see you, Leonora,' she repeated. 'Almost like the old days.'

'I noticed you stressed "almost",' the nurse said with a laugh, obviously trying to take Lisa's mind off the coming events. 'Welcome home, kid! I thought it might be you, Lisa, when they told us the name. All of five minutes ago,' she added ruefully. 'A good thing we're in a constant state of absolute readiness, eh?'

'Yeah. . .' Something of her usual calmness returned. Good old Leonora, always right on the ball.

'I didn't know you were pregnant. Long time no see, and all that.'

'It's a long story, Leonora.'

'Well, you're finally on the other side of the fence, eh?' All the time she was talking the nurse was attaching monitor leads to Lisa's chest, connecting her to a monitor that would automatically show and record her body's vital signs and the level of circulating oxygen in her blood-stream.

'Don't ask me what it's like. I'd rather be where you are,' Lisa said weakly, determined not to give way to panic.

'Well, don't you worry, honey. We're going to take real good care of you. We'll chat later. Now, they said in Emergency that you hadn't signed the consent to operation form yet. I know that you understand the nature of the operation that you're about to undergo so I'll just ask you to sign right here on the dotted line.'

It took a lot of concentration for Lisa to grasp the proffered pen and to sign her name on the form that was attached to a clipboard.

'We're not going to waste any time, Lisa. Your anaesthetist will be Rudy Frazer—he's new since you worked here. He's a really great guy—super at his job, great to talk to.' The nurse replaced the cap on the pen that she kept on a cord hanging round her neck.

'He'll be here to talk to you any second now, then we'll be wheeling you straight into the OR and ask you to climb onto the operating table before he actually gives the anaesthetic. That way, you won't be under the anaesthetic any longer than you possibly have to. We'll do the skin prep and put on the sterile drapes before you actually go under.'

'Yes.'

'I know you're familiar with the routine, honey,' Leonora said, 'but I always do the spiel anyway because I feel that if you break from routine, especially if it's a staff member, it's not good for the patient. So long as you know I'm not being patronizing, love.'

'Thanks, I appreciate that. You going to be the circulating nurse in there with me?'

'I sure am. Now. . .I understand you've got an empty stomach but, to be on the safe side, Dr Frazer will probably want to put down a gastric tube. He may do that while you're under the anaesthetic. Here comes Dr Frazer now. . .and the other guys are getting scrubbed.'

As another powerful contraction swept over her, Lisa was not able to suppress a moan of pain.

Leonora gripped her hand. 'Hang in there, honey. You'll be getting something for pain real soon. Everything's going to be just fine.'

She closed her eyes and rode out the pain with difficulty, trying to blot it out. Lisa felt her mind floating back to the time when she had worked in this unit, in the gynaecology and obstetrics OR. So much for trying to keep him out of her mind—it was impossible here. Because it was here that she had met Richard. . .all of two and a half years ago. . . Dr Richard Decker. As though she were still living in that time, she could clearly recall the sound of his voice, what he had said. . .

'Hi, there! And who might you be, you gorgeous creature? I thought they didn't come like that any more!'

Those had been the first words that Richard had said to her. Although she had tried to pretend to herself that she'd not been flattered, she had been kidding herself.

From the moment she'd turned to look at him she'd been smitten. She had never set eyes on him before, and she had been blissfully unaware of the momentous part he was to play in her young life.

'You're a welcome sight on a wet Monday morning, with a bloody great operating list ahead of us,' he'd said, looking at her with undisguised admiration. . .a look that she'd learnt later he'd perfected very well. It had been a look of burning intensity, as though the object of that intent regard had been the only thing that had mattered to him in the entire world. It had also been blatantly sexual. And it had had the effect of winding her, psychologically speaking.

It turned out that he was doing a six-month rotation as a resident in obstetrics and gynaecology, before starting his training in accident and emergency medicine at University Hospital. As she turned to look at him enquiringly in that first moment, to meet his penetrating green eyes which were regarding her with intense interest above the surgical mask that he wore, she experienced a peculiar shock, like a sense of recognition. Yet she had never seen him before in her life.

I must be desperate for a man, she thought musingly then. After the long, enforced deprivation, being away from civilization. . .

'What's your name?' he repeated, standing close to her and watching her work. He was very tall. The short-sleeved scrubsuit top that he wore did nothing to disguise the rippling muscles of his tanned arms. Almost then and there, she realized in retrospect, she had become infatuated with him.

'I'm Lisa Stanton,' she said, with feigned calm. 'I've been out of the country for a few weeks. I'm really an old hand.'

'I can see that you are,' he murmured, his voice deep

and caressing. After watching her for a few moments, during which his eyes seemed to bore into the small of her back, he said baldly, 'Are you spoken for?'

She stopped her activities. 'What? What do you mean?' she said.

'Have you got someone? Have you got a man?'

The atmosphere seemed charged with electricity as she stared at him in shocked silence while he stood tensely, watching her. Even then there was something proprietorial about him, as though he had a right to possess her. Only later had she seen it as predatory. With other men, so far, she had found that assumption annoying, sometimes laughable. Big egos were not always endearing. With this man it was suddenly overwhelmingly exciting, almost as though he had reached forward and touched her, taken possession of her.

'No. . .no, I haven't,' she found herself saying, as though the question were reasonable on a first meeting.

'Great!' he said, as though something were settled between them. 'I'm Richard Decker.'

'Hi,' she said.

By the end of that hectic day of gynaecological surgery Lisa felt that she knew a lot about Richard Decker—his prodigious ego, the immense driving force behind his capacity for work, his hard, clinical intelligence, his seductive charm. Because of her attraction to him she had overlooked the assumptions he had made which from someone else might have jarred.

'I've enjoyed working with you, Dr Decker.' She smiled at him sincerely. He had been more than competent.

'Call me Richard,' he said, when they were momentarily alone. 'Have dinner with me on the weekend. For once, I've got a whole weekend off. Who knows when it may happen again?'

'Well. . .' She hesitated, thinking of the essential chores

she usually did on the weekend, actually nervous about accepting his offer.

'Give me your phone number,' he said, grabbing a handy message pad and pen. 'I'll call you.'

Someone had come into the room then so she quickly gave him her number. With a tremor of delightful anticipation she felt that she had gone beyond a point of no return with him.

That was how it had begun—from a simple giving of her telephone number. From then on she would gradually give more to Dr Richard Decker. . .much, much more. And she hadn't, as it turned out, discovered as much about him on that first working day as she had thought.

'Is the pain bad?' The gentle question, spoken at her side, together with a spasm of pain brought her back abruptly to the present. In a few moments her mind had encompassed two and a half years of her past life.

Now the present intruded again forcefully as her eyelids shot open and she heard her own moan of pain—as though it were coming from another person—as her uterus contracted powerfully and another gush of fluid escaped from her body.

'Oh. . .the contractions are very strong,' she gasped, turning her head sideways. 'Please help me. . . The pain. . . I can't. . .'

'It's OK, everything's OK.'

Lisa's eyes met those of the gowned and masked figure beside her. Not for me, it isn't, she wanted to say to him. And maybe not for my baby, either.

'Hi! I've given you a shot of something in the IV. You should be feeling the effects of that any second now, just to take the edge off the pain,' he said. 'I'm Rudy Frazer, from the department of anaesthesia, and I'm going to be giving you your anaesthetic. Take a deep breath. . . Ride with the pain, if you can. That's it. . . Let it out slowly. In a moment or two I'm going to be giving you the Pentothal. OK? First, we're taking you into the OR.'

As he spoke he began to push the stretcher through a door into the room where she would have her operation. Turning her head, Lisa could see the large operating lights, already switched on, over the operating table. The scrub nurse was ready, standing waiting for her, with the surgeon and his two assistants. It was all so familiar. This time she was on the other side of the fence.

'Please. . .' Lisa looked up at Dr Frazer '. . .Don't let anything happen to this baby.'

'We won't,' Dr Rudy Frazer said emphatically. 'Now, just slide over there onto the operating table. That's my girl. . . Take the sheet with you. Great! Now, I want to ask you a few brief questions.'

She watched him take up the 20cc syringe that held the anaesthetic drug, Pentothal, that would put her to sleep in a few brief seconds when injected into her IV line. At the same time, the surgeons began prepping her abdomen with an iodine solution. The fear had receded somewhat now. From somewhere she had found the necessary strength. Leonora positioned her arms out on padded boards, moved her IV drip bags from the stretcher pole to another metal pole.

'Have you had an anaesthetic before? And are you allergic to any drugs that you know of?' Dr Frazer asked.

'No. . .no allergies. I've had an anaesthetic before when I had my appendix out at sixteen.'

'Great! Any problems with your heart, lungs or kidneys? Any major illnesses or blood-clotting problems?'

'No.'

'Right. Here we go, then, Lisa. First of all, I want you to breathe in a little more of the oxygen. . .just breathe normally.' As he placed a rubber mask over her mouth

Lisa decided that she liked Dr Frazer, that she trusted him implicitly. And he had a wonderful bedside manner. Out of the corner of her eye she saw his hands on the IV tubing, saw him position the needle of the syringe in one of the rubber ports.

For a second she felt a moment of panic, then Leonora was beside her, smiling calmly, reassuringly.

'Everything's going to be OK, Lisa.' Dr Frazer's soothing voice cut through her momentary fear. 'When you wake up you'll be in the recovery room. You'll probably still have a stomach tube in place. Not to worry about it. OK? Breathe away... Just concentrate on breathing...in and out...that's it.'

Unaccountably she thought of Marcus Blair as she listened to the calm, professional voice instructing her—she thought of his kindness, of the warmth of his hand. Would he be waiting for her as he had promised?

Then she felt herself sliding away, her eyelids heavy, the overhead lights blurred. 'Oh, my baby...my baby.' The anguished cry of longing broke from her. It was a primitive, instinctive cry from a need to protect her baby, in spite of her total helplessness. Now it was all out of her control—the whole situation. There was nothing she could do but trust those around her.

With all the fervour of her being she longed to hold that unseen baby in her arms, that baby that had already begun the epic journey of its life—the fight for survival. Like her, it had no alternative and because of that there was an unbreakable bond between them which would last for ever. She also shared a bond with all the women who had gone before her who had given birth from the dawn of human history, and with all the women who would come after her as long as the human race survived. With them, she risked her life.

'Marcus.' She whispered his name, the name of the man

whose image was in her brain now. He was the one who had been there for her when she so desperately needed someone. With an awful, sober clarity she knew now that that was what really mattered in the end.

'Sweet dreams,' someone said.

The words floated over her as she drifted into unconsciousness.

CHAPTER TWO

'YOU have a daughter, a beautiful daughter.'

The lights were very bright, throwing no shadows. As Lisa opened her eyes the people and things in the vast room seemed distanced from her, as though she were looking at it all through the wrong end of a telescope. People moved about here and there in front of her. Disorientated, she looked around her, not knowing where she was. She was propped up in a semi-sitting position on a stretcher.

A hand touched her cheek, gently moving her head round so that she found herself looking at a face that was very close—a man's face. 'Hi, I'm Marcus Blair. Remember me? It's all over. You're in the recovery room now,' the voice articulated slowly. 'Everything's fine. You've got a lovely girl. She's OK.'

Very slowly Lisa found herself coming back to a sense of time and place, of moving out of a momentary confusion. The remarkable thing about a general anaesthetic was that there was no awareness of the passage of time, not like a natural sleep. Now it seemed like a split second only had passed since she had seen Dr Rudy Frazer injecting the Pentothal into her IV tubing. Yet there was pain—of a different type—attesting to an unaccounted-for interval of time.

Over her nose and mouth a clear plastic mask delivered moistened oxygen. She could hear the bubbling of the vaporizer as her mind slowly identified the sights and sounds around her. There was a plastic airway in her mouth and Lisa found herself gagging on it. A hand reached forward to extricate it carefully from between her lips.

There was a peculiar taste in her mouth, coupled with the unmistakable odour of anaesthetic gases clinging to her.

Aware of tears running down her face, uncontrollable tears of abject relief, she focused on the man's face. He smiled, his teeth even and white. There was dark stubble on his chin and lower cheeks.

'Remember me?' he asked again, gently. 'Marcus?'

Lisa nodded, putting up a hand to lift the mask so that she could talk to him. 'Oh. . .yes, of course.' She smiled back tentatively. 'I'm so glad you're here. A. . .a girl?' Her throat felt dry, a little raw, and her speech was slurred.

'Yes. I've seen her. Not only is she beautiful, she's perfect—with ten toes and ten fingers, as well as everything else that she should have. And she's got a thatch of auburn hair, just like yours.'

'Oh. . .' she felt herself smiling that inane, relieved, delighted smile of the new mother—smiling at the miracle of creation, at the flood of maternal love and the surprise that it had all actually happened to her and the relief of finding herself still alive.

As her tear-filled eyes met his she really looked at him thoroughly for the first time now that there was all the time in the world, noticing how she could read the empathy and intelligence in his deep brown eyes. Intuitively she knew that he was a warm, loving man, one who would not stint in giving of himself yet, paradoxically, one who would not give himself thoughtlessly to a woman. A man who would only promise something after careful consideration of whether he could keep that promise. In other words, a man of integrity. There was an odd regret in her that she would not be that woman.

She could not have said how she knew those things—she just knew them. Perhaps she had matured in the past few months, would not so easily make the same mistakes again, she considered ruefully as her brain began to function again with a special clarity. At the same time she also knew instinctively that he was not like Richard, who would promise the earth and then not follow through. This man, Marcus Blair, would hold himself back until he knew for sure that he could follow through—that he would want to.

'Where is she. . .my baby?' Lisa whispered, looking into those warm brown eyes that held such an enigmatic, intriguing quality.

'She's in the premature baby unit right now, even though there's absolutely nothing wrong with her. She is premature, though, by dates if not by weight. She weighs eight pounds. I guess they'll keep her there for twenty-four hours, then she'll be in the general nursery where you are.'

'Are you sure she's all right?' Her eyes searched his face for any sign that he might be covering up something.

'Absolutely.'

'I had a feeling it would be a girl,' she whispered, smiling slowly. 'I think I wanted a girl. Of course, I don't mind either way, I'm so happy.'

Dazed, she swayed sideways. Marcus Blair put an arm around her shoulders as he stood next to the stretcher and steadied her, drawing her against him so that her head lolled against the side of his neck and she felt the comforting warmth of his skin against hers. That action and her acceptance of it brought a strange sense of added disorientation. . .that she should be held in this way by a man she scarcely knew. Somehow it seemed all right.

Then it registered with her that he was wearing the green regulation scrubsuit that the surgeons wore.

'They still think I'm your husband around here,' he explained, sensing her unasked questions. 'They also know I'm a doctor, due to start work in the emergency department here on the first day of January. That sure helped in getting me in here.'

'I'm very glad you did,' she murmured, breathing in

his male scent and the faint tang of a subtle cologne. As she relaxed against him she became aware of the pain of the operation increasing in intensity. Very soon it would be difficult to tolerate as the pain-killing effects of the anaesthetic rapidly wore off.

'I wish I could see her,' she said wistfully. 'I want to hold her so much.'

'You will. On the way to your floor, when you get out of here, you'll do a detour by the prem baby unit,' he assured her. 'Are you in pain now?'

'Yes. I. . .I feel as though I've been hit in the stomach with an axe.' The attempt to joke did not quite come off as the pain increased, tempering the wonderful exhilaration and relief she felt that the baby was alive and well.

'I'll speak to the nurse. They'll give you an injection of Demerol. Your mother's here, by the way, waiting on the floor where you'll be transferred. I called her after the baby was born so you'll be seeing her shortly.'

'Thank you. I'm immensely grateful,' she said, marvelling yet again at how incredibly lucky she had been in meeting him.

Yet at the time she had met Richard she had thought something similar about him, too, although for very different reasons. Then she had marvelled at the intense attraction between them which had seemed too good to be true. Could she really trust her first impressions when such things were often wrong? Much better to listen to one's instincts. Right now she knew that the dull, emotionally induced ache in the region of her heart was for Richard. . .for what might have been.

'Dr Blair. . .' She grasped his arm as he made to get up to call a nurse. 'I appreciate what you've done for me. If. . .if you have a wife I hope she understands what you're doing here.'

'I don't have a wife,' he said quietly, his eyes meeting hers again.

'Then you don't have any children of your own?' she asked, careful to keep her voice low. This was a strange conversation to be having with one's 'husband'. It was suddenly imperative that she know something of what he was all about. If he had had a wife, his presence with her would perhaps take on a bizarre quality.

'No, I have no children,' he said, getting up. 'I'll get a nurse to give you that Demerol.'

It was a relief to know that he was not married, otherwise she would feel that they were together somehow under false pretences because she was becoming used to him, perhaps just a little dependent on his quiet common sense.

When the nurse came Lisa was more than ready for the painkiller. So many emotions were churning within her mind. Not least was the concern about what Richard would think—or do—if he were to find out that she had given birth to his baby. Would he give a damn? Worse, would he think she had become pregnant in an attempt—a pathetic attempt, he would have said—to get him back?

'I understand your husband's going to be working in Emergency in the new year? Head of Department, eh?' the nurse said.

'Um. . .yes, that's right,' Lisa said, ad libbing, as she submitted to the jab of the needle.

Then she realized that if she were to get a post in the emergency department herself, as she hoped to do, she would be working with Dr Marcus Blair. That could lead to some complications if people there thought he was her husband. Perhaps by then anyone who knew about her delivery would have forgotten his presence. . .if she ever got a job there, which was by no means certain.

'Thanks.' Lisa smiled her gratitude at the nurse, trying

to take the advice to relax her body when it felt as though it had been pounded all over. With her eyes closed, she allowed the sounds of the room to wash over her. There were other patients all around her in various stages of recovery. Soon she would be wheeled on the stretcher up to the postnatal floor. On the way she would see her little girl. . .

'Hi.' A hand touched hers. 'I understand you've had that injection.' Dr Blair was back with her, sitting on a stool beside her stretcher.

'Yes. You. . .er. . .you look awfully tired. I feel really guilty, keeping you up,' she said quietly, apologetically, registering how exhausted he looked. His eyes were bloodshot. 'It must be the middle of the night. I've lost all sense of time.'

'Not quite the middle of the night,' he said lightly. 'Don't worry about it.'

'But I do worry about it,' she protested, 'when you've been so incredibly kind to me. Did you get a chance to have a meal?'

'Sure,' he said. 'I made a quick visit to the hospital cafeteria while you were under the anaesthetic. I'm fine.'

'I can feel the Demerol taking affect now,' she said drowsily. 'I. . .I'll probably see you around in the hospital some time in the new year. Hopefully, you won't have to rescue me again for anything.'

What she really wanted to ask was the question of whether she would ever see him again in a capacity other than a professional one. After the strange intimacy they had shared, during one of life's crises, it would be very odd to revert to a professional relationship. But, then, unless she got to work in Emergency it would perhaps not be a consideration. . .

'You'll take some months off, presumably?' he asked.

'Yes, three months' maternity leave. Then I'll be

coming back to work part time in the OR. . . or maybe the emergency department. . . I don't really know yet.'

'We may be colleagues, then,' he murmured.

'Maybe,' she agreed. 'I guess I'm lucky to be offered a part-time position in this economic recession.' Lisa stopped talking, aware that she was prattling on because Marcus Blair was sitting very close to her, watching her in a very astute way. Suddenly there was a tension between them which she felt acutely, even though the edge of her awareness was rapidly becoming dulled by the drug she had received.

Maybe he was wondering what sort of person he had really got himself temporarily involved with, she thought—maybe wondering whether there would be any negative repercussions for him. He must surely be wondering why she didn't want Richard informed.

'I've been talking to your mother,' he said. 'She told me you have a flat in their house. . .your childhood home.'

'Yes,' she said.

'Maybe I shouldn't ask this,' he said slowly, 'but I'm going to, anyway. I'm curious. Tell me to go to hell if you want. What about the guy. . .Richard?'

There was no point in prevaricating. Lisa moistened her dry lips. 'He's out of the picture,' she said softly. 'I don't intend to tell him I have a baby.'

'Your mother doesn't seem to think he's out of the picture,' he said.

'Well. . .' She fought to concentrate as her thinking processes became fuzzy. 'She. . .she harbours a hope that we'll get married, that everything will be OK between us. It's too late for that, all over. . .' Her speech had become slurred and she closed her eyes wearily.

'So you don't want him contacted?'

'No.'

'Look, I'm going to go now. You need to sleep.'

'Must you?' she whispered.

'No. . .not if you don't want me to.'

'Mr Stanton, your wife's doing too much talking, I think, and not breathing in enough of that oxygen.' The nurse took the decision out of her hands. 'Maybe it's time for you to go, if you wouldn't mind. You can see her later on the postnatal ward. OK?' It was an outright dismissal.

From under heavy lids Lisa watched Marcus stand up, ready to leave. 'Yes, yes, of course,' he agreed.

All at once she wanted to howl, to articulate her need of him, to put her arms around his neck and hold him tightly to her. Or was it really Richard she wanted? There was so much confusion in her tired mind.

Once again he pressed her hand briefly as the nurse moved away from them. 'Goodbye, Lisa,' he said softly. 'Take care of yourself and that lovely baby.'

Lisa returned the pressure, hoping he would understand from that simple gesture the depth of her gratitude. How inadequate it seemed. 'Goodbye, Marcus,' she whispered.

She kept her eyes closed while he walked away from her, holding her breath on the sob that rose uncontrollably to her throat. Now she had the double loss to bear—the loss of her baby from her womb and now the loss of the man who had somehow helped her to hold herself together.

The longing for her baby, that tiny scrap of humanity, was acute. Somewhere in the hospital, in the premature baby unit, she, too, was essentially alone. Lisa had the poignant urge to get up and run to her. What if everyone had been lying and she had not survived? Until she saw for herself she could not still the underlying feeling of agitation, even though the powerful drug was having its effect.

Perhaps if she gave the baby a name it would help. Emma, perhaps. . .or Kate? Those were two of the names she had considered for a girl. Lily? Ruth? Katya? Her tired brain considered all the names. Why not Emma Kate? Yes, that was it! Hullo, Emma Kate. She sent a silent message to her baby, as though by sheer will-power she could communicate. I'll be with you very soon.

Although she was not physically isolated or alone—far from it in that bustling room—and was very well taken care of, she felt herself to be an island, washed on all sides by a vast, lonely ocean with nothing else in sight as far as the eye could see.

'You have the most beautiful blue eyes I have ever seen,' Richard had said on that very first dinner date they had spent together on that first weekend.

'Are you flattering me with any specific purpose in mind?' she had responded lightly.

'Sure I am.' He had grinned back. 'What else?' Although he'd said it without any particular inflection, there had been an unmistakable message there. Now I think I know where I stand, she had thought. But she had been more innocent than she had supposed then.

Perhaps she should have backed off, should not have picked up the challenge. Even then she had begun to understand that Dr Richard Decker had seldom done anything—or said anything—without a purpose, without making a move towards something he wanted. Where she should have been warned, she'd found his assumptions somehow exhilarating. Against her better judgement, she had picked up the gauntlet, so to speak.

After six months they had been living together. . .

'We're going to take you up to the floor now, Mrs Stanton.' A voice cut through her jumbled reverie. This time there was a sense that time had passed, that she had slept. 'All your vital signs are normal so we're going to ship you out.' The same nurse who had given the injection was back.

'Thanks.' Lisa smiled.

'Has the pain gone?' the nurse asked.

'Yes,' Lisa mumbled, 'I feel fine now. Will I be able to see my baby on the way?'

'You sure will. I'll be going with you.'

'Here she is, Mrs Stanton. All eight pounds of her!'

Emma Kate was wrapped in a pale pink blanket, bundled up neatly like a parcel so that only her head was showing.

'Can I. . . Can I hold her?'

'You sure can.' The nurse in the premature baby unit handed over the pink bundle which was surprisingly heavy.

Reaching for her daughter, Lisa knew that she was going to cry. There was no holding back the emotion that welled up in her.

'They all cry!' the nurse said in mock resignation. 'It must be something to do with the separation. She sure is a cute one!'

'Oh. . .she's so sweet, so beautiful,' Lisa whispered as, with blurred vision, she surveyed her baby for the first time. Then she lifted the face up to hers to feel the velvet-soft skin against her own, to feel the fine, downy hair.

Emma Kate had her eyes closed, her face in repose. Her eyelids were a little puffy and her face with its soft, full cheeks a little tired, signifying the fraught journey she had endured to get into the outside world. As her heart contracted with love and empathy Lisa kissed her daughter. There seemed to be nothing of Richard in her daughter's face. In fact, she seemed to look like her maternal grandmother, the same soft, very feminine persona.

Somewhat fearfully Lisa had wondered whether she would love her child any less if it looked exactly like

Richard. . .even though she still loved him. Now she knew that none of that mattered.

'We'll bring her for you to feed in the morning.' The nurse took Emma Kate back. 'Then after twenty-four hours you'll have her with you.'

'Thank you.'

CHAPTER THREE

THE mirror showed a face that was considerably thinner than it had been a few weeks previously. There were hollows in the cheeks, shadows under the eyes.

'I look exhausted.' Lisa spoke out loud, addressing her reflection in her bathroom mirror. 'I am exhausted.'

Looking at herself critically, she saw a face which was abnormally pale after weeks of winter. Also, there was no denying that she had matured, that a certain plump, dewy youthfulness had gone, perhaps for ever. Lisa peered closer into her own eyes. She was not sorry that she had changed. After all, a woman in her mid-twenties should be grown up. It was time to stop mulling over pointless regrets about the past. There was nothing like a baby to force you to put your own ego on hold, to take a leap towards maturity.

''Morning, Lisa, I thought I heard you moving about.'

'Oh, hullo, Mum,' Lisa said, turning to look at her mother who had come to stand in the open door of her bathroom, wearing an old dressing-gown that had seen better days. 'I hope we didn't wake you. The baby's asleep again. I was up at six. . .she slept a little later this morning.'

'Good. You certainly need your sleep.' Mrs Stanton, like her daughter, had thick auburn hair, hers interspersed with grey, tied behind her head with a piece of ribbon.

Impulsively, Lisa moved forward and gave her mother a quick, appreciative hug. 'You shouldn't have got up,' she admonished. 'My appointment isn't until ten. I can manage until then.'

'I know.' Her mother smiled. 'I was awake, anyway.'

'I hope Dad didn't wake up?'

'No. You know, Lisa, I can't help thinking that maybe you shouldn't return to work tomorrow. Maybe you should have another month off.'

'You and Dad have done enough for me,' Lisa said decisively, moving towards the kitchen of her small flat that formed part of her parents' old, rambling house which had been her home since early childhood. 'And now that my maternity pay has just about run out I don't want you to be supporting me financially as well.'

'You're our daughter,' her mother said simply. 'What we have is yours. I wouldn't want it any other way.'

'I know. I appreciate that. It's just that I don't want to impose on you. And I've got some financial catching up to do. Tea, Mum? Or coffee?'

'Coffee will be fine.'

'If you start doing too much for me I shall have to keep that connecting door closed,' Lisa said lightly, teasingly, referring to the door between her own self-contained flat and the rest of the house.

'What time are you seeing that nice Dr Blair?' Mrs Stanton asked as she got two mugs out of a cupboard.

'After the hairdresser, to have my unruly locks chopped off, I'm going to come back here, feed Emma and then go to the hospital to see him at three o'clock,' Lisa said, feeling a quick pang of anticipation at the prospect of seeing Marcus Blair again. They had not met since the birth of the baby, although she had spoken to him on the telephone. . .twice.

'I still can't get over how wonderful he was to you,' her mother said. 'Such a charming, yet forthright sort of man. Aren't you glad you'll be working with him?'

'Yes, I think I am,' Lisa said thoughtfully as she spooned ground coffee into an automatic coffee-maker. 'I'm also wondering whether I'll feel any sort of embarrassment. I was *in extremis* when he saw me. Worse... he might feel embarrassed,' Lisa confessed, thinking of Marcus Blair hovering behind the inadequate curtains in the emergency department cubicle while she'd had a urinary catheter inserted and her blood-stained clothing removed.

'I shouldn't think so,' her mother said. 'He seemed to me to be a very sophisticated sort of man. It's all in a day's work for him, anyway, isn't it?'

'Mmm. . .maybe,' Lisa said thoughtfully. 'Maybe not. Anyway, I'll sure be glad when this interview's over. I'm not quite sure why he wants to see me, anyway. The head nurse said he asked especially to see me before I started work. I mean. . .it's not usual. Nurses are hired—and interviewed—by nurses, not by doctors.'

'Maybe he's doing it just so that you *won't* feel any embarrassment when you first come face to face with each other in a work setting. That's my guess, Lisa. Don't worry about it. You've definitely got the job in the emergency department, haven't you?'

'Yes. Sadie Drummond—that's the head nurse—told me she'd be very pleased to have me work four days a week, five hours each day, from early morning,' Lisa said, pouring them both coffee.

'There you are, then,' her mother said decisively. 'I just hope it won't be too much for you, that's all.'

So—privately—did Lisa. Basically, she had never been so exhausted in her life. 'I'll be OK,' she assured her mother. 'If it proves to be too much I'll just take on less, that's all.'

Mrs Stanton stood up, holding her mug of coffee. 'I'll come to babysit at about nine-thirty,' she said.

'That's great,' Lisa said, standing up and kissing her mother on the cheek—appreciating her mother's sensitivity to her need for privacy and independence ever since she had moved back to her old flat here in her parents' home after the awful break-up with Richard. . .

When her mother had gone Lisa took her mug of coffee upstairs into the small second bedroom to check once again on her daughter. The truth is, she acknowledged as she bent over the cot that held her sleeping daughter, I don't really want to leave her.

Emma lay on her side with her eyes closed, wrapped in a quilt. Her long, dark eyelashes fanned down onto her soft, full cheeks. A shock of dark auburn hair fringed her forehead. When she awoke she would smile—that slow, gummy, delighted smile that she had just started to give in the past week when she focused on her mother—her large blue eyes shining. There was something very, very positive about a baby.

'I never knew,' Lisa whispered, 'that it was possible to love someone so much.' It was different from the love for a man. When would it register with her daughter, she wondered sadly, that she had no father? How many years would it take? And would it matter as much as she thought it might?

It was good to be back in the flat, her old home. It wasn't tainted with memories of Richard. How desperately she had wanted to come back here after the debacle of the last time she had set eyes on Richard—the night she had become pregnant with Emma Kate. She sipped the hot coffee, remembering against her will. . .

The apartment, in the smart new apartment block, that she'd shared with Richard had been in an awful mess that night when a key had turned in the lock just as she'd been packing the last of her books into small, manageable cardboard cartons.

She'd been in a mess too, wearing a robe over her underwear. Richard had essentially already moved out at that point, the break-up complete. Already he had told her that there was another woman, that he'd wanted 'out' of the relationship. . .as he had so unromantically put it. Not that there was anything she had *done*, he had said—or anything she had not done, come to that.

She had been kneeling on the floor, her hands full of books, when he had walked into the living room.

'Hi,' he said nonchalantly. 'How goes it?' He spoke as though they hadn't had the acrimonious break-up, as though she hadn't been almost paralytic with shock and was only now accepting the reality that he no longer wanted to live with her.

'Oh. . .just about finished,' she said, finding her voice. 'I. . .I was just wondering what to do with the few things you left behind. Is that why you're here?'

When he stood looking at her—sizing her up, so to speak—maybe she should have guessed what was to come. But she didn't guess.

Richard looked very attractive—tall, heavily masculine, casually dressed in blue jeans and check shirt under a lightweight jacket, which he shrugged out of quickly.

'Yeah, just came to pick it up, actually,' he said, still seeming quite at ease while she had struggled to display some semblance of calm. 'I believe I left a suitcase here as well.'

'Yes, you did. Several,' Lisa said.

'I've missed you,' he said unexpectedly.

'I can't believe that,' she said, hoping he couldn't see how much of an effort the words cost her. You couldn't switch love on and off at will, even when you knew for sure that someone was no good for you.

The bedroom was in a shambles where she had piled what remained of his stuff in one corner, together with his bags. Going ahead of him into that room, where the bed had been dismantled and the mattress pushed to one side against a wall, Lisa indicated with a sweep of her arm his pile of belongings.

'That's all your stuff,' she said.

'It's true,' he persisted, taking her by the arms and looking into her eyes in the way that she had in the past found irresistible, 'that I've missed you. You can't sleep with someone for a whole year and not miss them.'

'Can't you, Richard? Is that all it's meant to you?' Her voice trembled, tinged with bitterness. The last thing she wanted to be was bitter, a destructive emotion she had so often seen in others.

'I can't pretend that I didn't want to get my hands on you the moment I saw you,' he said. 'That wasn't all of it.' He pulled her against him as he spoke.

'If you expect me to be magnanimous, you're mistaken,' she had said as calmly as she could. 'I can't pretend that I don't care.'

'You think it's easy for me?' he said roughly.

'You're the one who's going,' Lisa said tartly. She pulled away from him, feeling the old familiar weakening of her will when he was close to her. One day. . . perhaps. . .she would get over him.

Together they packed up his clothes, the few medical books and personal effects that he had left behind when he had taken the bulk of his things days before. Lisa folded his shirts and sweaters with exaggerated care, not wanting him to see any display of anger on her part. Perhaps she also wanted to delay the inevitable parting, after which she expected not to see him again. Inside, she had been weeping.

They were both kneeling beside the mattress when the packing was completed. She looked up to see him staring at her bare thigh where the robe had gaped open.

'Can't we be friends, Lisa?' he said. 'Who knows. . . maybe one day we could get together again?'

At that moment she so wanted the possibility to be there that a wild hope made her heart rate accelerate, even though the sober voice of reason whispered to her that they had never really been friends. At least, he had never had her best interests at heart—had simply taken all that she had to give, had finally made her feel that it was not enough and had made her feel inadequate.

He kissed her, with all the passion of their first liaison, taking her by surprise. At first she resisted, then found her loneliness giving way to his compelling charm.

'Don't shut me out.' He breathed the words into her ear, even though he had been the one to walk out.

In seconds he had pulled her down onto the mattress and had moved his weight to pin her down. Winded, she lay there, unable to summon up the necessary energy to move. The warmth of his body renewed the crazy hope in her.

'It's not you, Lisa,' he said thickly, his mouth brushing hers, 'it's me. I can't seem to stay with a woman for longer than about a year. I guess I don't want to be tied down... not yet. The other won't last, either. At least I'm not going to live with her.'

Before she could think of a suitable retort, her painful thoughts in chaos, he was kissing her hungrily—not like a man who had dismissed her from his life so summarily three weeks before. She struggled at first.

'No... I don't think this is a good idea,' she protested weakly, while her body betrayed her.

'Lisa... Lisa, I still want you,' he murmured. 'Maybe there's a future for us.'

'How can you want me?' she managed to gasp out, feeling herself weakening in the face of his undoubted physical attraction which she had never been able to resist. He knew just how to handle her, knew her responses intimately.

'I just do. I'm a bastard, I know it,' he said. Then they rolled together to the centre of the bed. Helplessly she found herself responding to him, telling herself as she did so that it was wrong for her. For a few moments only she knew that she would regret this. Then the physical reality of him dominated her mind, her emotions, as he made love to her quickly and furiously. It was like it always had been with them.

To his credit, afterwards he did not leave her immediately. He made coffee for them both, stayed long enough to tidy the apartment with her and bring it to some semblance of order. It was long enough for her hope not to die completely.

Before he left he didn't ask her whether she was still taking the Pill. She had been taking it, yet in her emotional state she might have forgotten a day or two. . . She didn't think so.

Six weeks later she knew for sure that she was pregnant. By that time she also knew that he was not coming back. She found out quickly that there was nothing like a pregnancy to make stark reality assert itself.

At a quarter to three that afternoon Lisa was at University Hospital. It was not the first time she had been there since the baby was born—she had been there for postnatal check-ups and to have an interview with the head nurse of the emergency department, Sadie Drummond, before she had definitely got her job there.

She was going to miss the operating room, she acknowledged as she walked briskly along a familiar corridor leading from a main entrance, but there was no way she could work part time there.

The knowledge that she was to meet Dr Marcus Blair again in a few minutes made her unusually flustered, even though she knew that she looked attractive, smart and businesslike in her dark suit and silk scarf, topped by a gabardine trench coat against the early spring chill. Her hair, cut short, formed a shining cap of dark auburn.

The emergency department did not appear to be humming with activity when she got there. As she passed the main waiting room she could see that there were only two people in it. Then suddenly there he was, Marcus Blair, at the other end of the corridor, walking towards her as she made her way to where she knew the office of the head of department to be. In her imagination she had seen herself knocking at his door, waiting for a quiet command to enter and had mentally rehearsed what she would say and do once in there. She would be all composed and serene, not concentrating on the unusual relationship they had shared three months before.

Now here he was, with all the time in the world to size her up, and her rehearsed scenes disappeared like the proverbial dew before the sun as her heart gave a nervous leap. She had forgotten how very attractive he was. Or perhaps, more accurately, she had not been in a state to really notice. . .

He wore a white lab coat over grey trousers that emphasized his long legs and a white shirt, open at the neck. His dark hair was a little longer than she had remembered it and ruffled, as though he had run his hands through it. He looked tanned and very fit, as if he had recently been away somewhere for a vacation. His eyes, dark and penetrating, were as she remembered, she saw as he got closer. While she stood waiting for him he fixed those eyes on her face and kept them there. He walked languidly, taking his time.

'Well. . . Lisa Stanton, right on time.' He reached her and held out a hand. 'How are you?' He smiled slightly, his astute eyes going over her—seeming to take in every minute detail about her and read her mind as well.

'I. . .I'm well, thank you,' she said, taking his hand and wondering why she was having difficulty getting her tongue round those simple words—why her carefully rehearsed introduction had deserted her.

All she could think of then was that he had kissed her when he had pretended to be her husband and that, shockingly, she wanted him to kiss her now—to enfold her in his arms in the way that he had done before when she had so needed him. . .as though she had a right.

The thought brought colour to her cheeks, which she strove to suppress. Of course she had no right. For a few seconds, as she returned his intense scrutiny, she felt he knew exactly what she wanted from him. That knowledge made her vulnerable.

'How are you, Dr Blair?' she asked quickly. 'I. . .I hope you're enjoying your new job here?' From now on she had to be careful with men. Now she was a mother she was no longer free in the same way.

'Oh, yes, I'm enjoying it very much.' he said, his warm, slow drawl causing the colour in her cheeks to deepen.

Lisa found herself smiling. It was uncommonly good to see him and she found herself hoping fervently that it would last when they were working together.

'And how's that beautiful baby?' he asked, opening the door of his office and motioning her to enter.

'She's lovely.' Lisa could hear her own voice taking on a softer note. 'Healthy, well-behaved—most of the time—and still very beautiful. I adore her.'

'I can see that you do. Let me take your coat,' he said. 'Perhaps you'll let me see her some time.'

'Yes, of course.' Her heart gave a leap of pleasure. Did he really mean it, or was he just being polite? Oddly, she thought she could detect a reticence in him that belied his interest.

She slipped out of her raincoat. For a few seconds his

hands rested on her shoulders as he helped her with it, and she found herself excessively sensitive to his nearness, tensing.

'I'll keep you to that,' he said softly, hanging her coat up on a hook. 'I've often thought about you both.'

'I. . .I shall never forget your kindness,' she said, stammering a little. In fact, over the past three months she had thought of Marcus Blair as much as she had thought of Richard. What she had so needed was Dr Blair's particular brand of kindness. What she had received from Richard during their time together was something much more common—she could admit that now.

'Please sit down, Lisa.' He indicated a comfortable chair, one of two, that was positioned next to a small coffee-table, apart from a large desk that was piled with papers. He took the other chair close to hers. 'Do you mind if I call you by your first name?'

'Oh, no. . .no,' she said.

This was perhaps not going to be as easy as she had hoped. Already she felt a little out of her depth with him now that their relationship was shifting to a professional one. Perhaps he was trying to redress a balance, to distance her. There were vibes between them that she could not place.

'Luckily, we're not busy here right now,' he said, 'although all hell could break loose any minute. I had two myocardial infarcts in this morning and one diabetic who hadn't taken his insulin on time. Everything else was pretty minor.'

Obviously he was trying to put her at her ease so Lisa made a determined effort to relax. He was certainly a very attractive man, almost alarmingly so—the sort of doctor who had every female in his vicinity hanging onto his every word and going out of their way to interact with him. She had seen it all before, and she didn't want to join the crowd. Yet, inevitably, she felt drawn to him.

'Why exactly did you want to see me, Dr Blair?' she said. 'I assume that my job here is assured?' She stopped, looking down at her clasped hands—trying to find a balance between the strictly professional and the personal feelings evoked by the memories of him.

'I wanted to make sure,' he began quietly, looking her full in the face, 'that there's no awkwardness between us when we start working together. I wanted to test the waters, so to speak. For me there is no awkwardness, Lisa. You were the one who had to go through it all. So far, I haven't met anyone in the hospital who has asked me how my wife and baby are. . .so maybe there isn't going to be any explaining to do on that issue.'

'I'm relieved about that,' she said. 'It could be. . .a little difficult to explain away. I suppose if we just told the truth that would be it.'

'Yes. . .' He was smiling slightly, his expression unreadable. 'I wanted to let you know that I thought you very brave that night. At the time I wanted to say it but there just didn't seem to be the right opportunity.'

'You helped me to be brave,' she said simply.

'I'm glad about that,' he said, seeming at ease. 'I thought I'd also take the opportunity to learn something about your nursing background. I know that isn't usual practice. It might help us to revert to a. . .more professional relationship.'

'I see,' she said. So that was really why he wanted to see her—to place her in a professional context.

'I thought I would also give you something of *my* professional background since you have to work with me as your medical boss—although Sadie Drummond is very much *the* boss.' He stood up. 'Let me get you a cup of coffee.'

'Thank you.'

There was an automatic coffee-making machine in the room, with the jug already full of aromatic coffee. As he poured for them both her eyes strayed to his broad back, his dark hair, his competent hands. She liked the unhurried way he did things.

Not as tall or as aggressively male as Richard, there was something about him—a strength, a manliness, understated—that impressed and unsettled her. He would be something to contend with, complex and perceptive—she knew that instinctively. And her mother was right—he was a sophisticated man.

'Cream and sugar, Lisa?'

'Please.'

As he handed her the cup, standing close, Lisa felt the tension increase and her throat close up.

'My background is in general and chest surgery, plus accident and emergency training,' he began, having taken mouthfuls of coffee. 'For various reasons, I've decided to concentrate on emergency work, mainly because it's what interests me the most. I've had experience in trauma surgery in central Canada, near the Rockies, and what you could call the gateway to the North. . .and in Africa.'

Lisa swallowed. 'Africa!' She was immediately more alert. 'I've been to Africa myself with the nursing branch of International Physicians. Were you. . .were you with them?' Sparkling with excitement, she turned in her chair towards him and leaned forward.

'Yes, I was. How extraordinary!' Dr Blair was looking at her as though she had taken on a new dimension for him—as though, Lisa thought, she was not just an ordinary nurse who had had the lack of common sense to allow herself to become pregnant at the wrong time with the wrong man.

'I've been in Ethiopia and Somalia,' she said enthusiastically. 'They wanted me to go to Rwanda but I. . .

couldn't go.' That was when she had been involved with Richard.

'I see,' he said evenly.

Then, with a few well-chosen sentences, she filled him in about her training and professional background.

'It was here that you met Dr Richard Decker?' he suddenly asked.

'Um. . .yes,' she answered haltingly. 'He. . .he was a senior obstetrics resident then.' Lisa looked down at her hands holding the coffee-cup, willing them not to shake.

When he remained silent she looked at him, to find him watching her. Desperate to change the subject, she asked, 'Were you in Rwanda, Dr Blair?' It was an educated guess as there was an air of strain about him now, as though memories had been stirred.

'Yes. I take jobs in Canada where I can be released to go where I'm needed overseas. . .at relatively short notice.'

'Was it. . .awful?'

'Like something out of a nightmare,' he said.

'I can imagine,' she murmured, remembering. 'I worked at casualty stations. . . They were called the "surgical pits", as I guess you know. Very apt.'

'Don't regret not going there. Maybe it's just as well that you didn't go. Basically, as a species, we're a savage lot.' There was an edge of bitter cynicism in his voice.

'Does that tell you something about me?' she asked with a certain challenge in her tone, looking up to find his intent eyes on her again.

'I believe it does,' he said.

Again the atmosphere crackled with an emergent tension. Against her will she was forced to recognize it. She had wanted to remain emotionally sober, withdrawn from the world of adult man-woman relationships, since the birth of her baby. It afforded a breathing space. Yet she could not deny that she found Marcus Blair strangely disturbing, even though she still had feelings for Richard.

'I know I shouldn't ask this,' he said, putting down his cup. 'It's against the labour-relations rules, or something. . . Are you going to be able to manage working here and looking after a baby? An emergency department can be very demanding, very stressful.'

'I've thought all that out, Dr Blair,' she said firmly, 'and I'm probably more fortunate than most women in my position. Both my parents are very supportive—I have a flat in their home. My mother is a commercial artist, working at home, and she's going to babysit. When it gets too much for her we'll get a nanny.'

'I see,' he murmured.

'Of course, I shan't want to leave the baby, but it is part time. You needn't worry, Dr Blair, that I won't be concentrating on the job while I'm here.'

'I'll take your word for it,' he said smoothly. 'And what about Dr Richard Decker?'

'I. . .haven't seen him for a long time. . .about a year.'

To her relief, someone knocked on the door at that moment.

'Come in,' Dr Blair said.

A nurse put her head round the office door. 'You're not going to believe this, Dr Blair,' she said, having given Lisa a quick glance. 'We have what looks very much like another myocardial infarct, and there's a head injury on the way by ambulance, a sub-arachnoid haemorrhage—a young guy fell off a bicycle. There's a woman on her way with a possible ruptured ectopic pregnancy, sent by her GP. I've got the gynae resident onto that. The waiting room's filling up, too, with the usual minor stuff.'

'Thanks. I'll be with you in a moment,' he said, standing up. When the nurse had gone he turned to Lisa. 'One more thing, Lisa. Have you told Richard Decker that you have a baby?'

Stunned into telling the absolute truth, she blurted out, 'No. No, I haven't.'

'Are you planning to?'

'I. . . No.'

'Perhaps it's none of my business. . .but don't you think you ought to?' The look he gave her seemed to carry censure in it, as well as a certain wariness.

Struck dumb, Lisa had no idea what to say.

'Well, goodbye for now, Lisa,' he said crisply, looking at her astutely with those penetrating dark eyes. 'I have to go. See you in the department tomorrow.'

With that he was gone, leaving Lisa realizing that she was holding her breath and feeling as though she had been through some sort of cathartic experience. Inwardly she was trembling. He certainly didn't waste time in circuitous questioning.

It had turned out that she and Dr Blair had a lot in common, yet at the same time there was something about him that was closed and mysterious. There had been no hint about his personal life.

And what she had not told him about herself was that her experiences in Africa, the things she had seen there, had made her very vulnerable to the normality that Richard Decker had seemed to offer when she had come back to University Hospital. She had embraced that normality. . . and him. Neither could she have told Marcus Blair that Richard had made no attempt to get in touch with her after he had so blatantly used her. That dismissal had served to reinforce what she already knew.

A poignant sadness came to her then in the empty room. It would be a long time before she felt free to care for another man, a long time before she could trust again. Would any other man want her with another man's child? Emma Kate was now the centre of her life. The blood-tie could never be broken. She didn't want it to be broken.

CHAPTER FOUR

'WHATEVER you do in this department never give out your real name to the patients who come in here,' Sadie Drummond, the head nurse, was saying emphatically to the two listening nurses. 'Never, ever! Don't forget it! And that applies to your first name and your surname. On your hospital ID badge you will have the first name—and the first name only—that you choose to be known by while you are on duty here.'

'Is it as bad as that?' The other nurse, who was with Lisa on her first day, looked at the head nurse as though she did not believe her.

'It is. We get the dregs of the earth in here, like you wouldn't believe! Not the majority of them. . .but enough to make life here definitely unsafe. We've had our fair share of stalkers, targeting nurses, so unless you want some guy on your back—literally, sometimes—you'll take my advice.'

The three of them were standing in the main reception lobby of the emergency department, where several sets of glass doors swung open every few seconds to admit people, some walking and some on stretchers, together with a touch of early spring air which mingled with the faint scent of petrol fumes from the waiting ambulances outside. The hum of activity was distracting. It was through those doors that Lisa had been brought on a stretcher three months before—she would never forget it.

Sadie Drummond, large-boned, plain-speaking and very competent, was orientating her two new nurses to the department. The interruptions were rampant, yet she soldiered on.

'Let's get out of here into my office and have a cup of coffee,' she said, turning away from the busy scene at the door and striding down a side passage, with the two nurses following her. It was ten o'clock in the morning.

'You'll both start off working in the reception area where we do the assessments when the patients first come in.' She continued talking as she moved. 'That's where we separate the ambulatory patients from the more serious cases. Then you'll gradually work your way through all areas of the department so that at the end of your three-week orientation period you will know precisely how each part of the system works. Later on you'll be assigned to an area where any previous experience you've had can be put to good use.'

She swept into a small cubby-hole which was her office. 'You, Miss Stanton,' she said, 'I shall probably put to work in one of our small operating rooms because of your extensive OR experience.'

Lisa nodded, giving Miss Drummond her full attention. They had been in the department since half-past seven that morning, and already it seemed to Lisa that she had put in a full day's work. The emergency department was unpredictable.

'We do things like tracheostomies there, and the treatment of gunshot wounds, as well as the stabilization process for the road-traffic accident cases and other accidents before the patients get transferred to the main operating room or the intensive care unit. We do a lot of intubations and the insertion of chest tubes for crushing injuries, fractured ribs, and so on,' Miss Drummond said.

Lisa nodded enthusiastically, already looking forward to the challenging work that she knew lay ahead. 'I should like that,' she said.

'Help yourself to coffee,' Sadie Drummond said, indicating her coffee-maker on a side table. While the two nurses moved to comply she went on talking, filling them in about the workings of the department.

Lisa glanced sideways at the other woman, Diane Crane, RN, who was a little older than she was herself. Diane grinned slightly. They were both very impressed with Sadie Drummond.

'Of course,' Miss Drummond went on relentlessly, 'you will have to be competent in—and be prepared to work in—any part of the department at a moment's notice. Every few months you will be expected to do a rotation through all the areas, just to keep your hand in. We get a lot of cardiac arrests here.'

A young intern poked his head round the open doorway.

'Excuse me, Miss Drummond,' he said reverently, his tones soft, 'Dr Claibourne's here and he wants to have a word with you.'

'That man!' Sadie Drummond expostulated. 'Why does a perfectly competent surgeon always want his hand held the minute he gets down here? Eh? Why can't he just get on with things, just do what he's told, like the rest of them?'

The intern made no comment, just smiled.

'Excuse me, girls.' The head nurse expressed regret. 'I'll be back in about fifteen minutes, which should just give me long enough to strangle that Dr Jerry Claibourne. Take a coffee-break.'

For a few seconds after her departure the two nurses sipped their coffee in silence, then Diane Crane looked at Lisa and they both erupted into uncontrollable laughter.

'I can't imagine any stalker getting on her back, can you?' Diane spluttered.

'No, I bet she's a self-defence expert,' Lisa agreed,

knowing that she was going to like the department very much.

'Yeah, hand-to-hand combat, I should think.'

'Sounds like we're going to need it here.'

They both wore white uniform pants suits and the regulation white shoes. Where Lisa was auburn-haired and full-breasted, Diane was fair-haired and skinny, her arms almost as thin as a child's.

'I've worked in emergency departments before,' Diane said, 'but nothing as big as this, or as busy, and not in an inner city area either.'

'I bet you're not as fragile as you look, Diane.' Lisa smiled at the other woman, sensing that they were going to have a good working relationship and perhaps becoming good friends.

'No, I'm not, although sometimes it's convenient to let the male sex think so,' Diane said succinctly. 'Talking of men, what do you think of the head of department. . .Dr Blair? It's a long time since I've seen such a gorgeous-looking guy, who also seems pretty decent as well. I guess it's too much to hope for that he isn't married.'

'Um. . .I think he's a very nice person, and a good doctor. I don't know him very well.' That was true, Lisa told herself, not wishing to deceive the other woman and yet not wanting her to pick up any hints that she had anything special going with Dr Blair. After all, she didn't, did she? 'I do happen to know that he isn't married.'

'Wow!' Diane said, opening her eyes wide in appreciation. 'I could sure weave a few fantasies around him!'

'Yes,' Lisa agreed thoughtfully, 'I second that.'

'Well, Lisa, what name are you going to give yourself on your ID badge? I thought I'd call myself Anne. At least the other nurses will know my real name.'

'I could call myself Liz, I guess. That's about the closest to my real name.'

'Come with me, girls.' Sadie Drummond was back. 'I've shown you the main waiting area for the ambulatory patients, the reception and the assessment areas. Now we're going to take a look at the treatment cubicles for the stretcher cases, then our three small operating/resuscitation rooms for our accident cases. I may have to leave you to your own devices very shortly. Things are hotting up around here.'

Hastily the two nurses put down their coffee-cups and followed her out. The whole place was humming with activity. Stretchers, wheelchairs, ambulatory patients and staff weaved around each other in a kind of controlled, urgent dance. Ambulance drivers and paramedics were issuing instructions to each other as they came and went.

'This is sure different from the way it was yesterday,' Lisa confided as they all set a brisk pace to the stretcher cubicles.

'This is more like normal,' Miss Drummond stated flatly. 'We're going into a crisis room. Patient with an overdose of drugs—street drugs, probably heroin. I'm going to be helping here so you stay well out of the way and just watch for now.'

As they walked quickly down a wide passage to the treatment area for stretcher cases three doctors, all wearing scrubsuits, operating caps and masks, came out of one of the operating rooms.

Diane nudged Lisa as they walked. 'There he is,' Diane hissed. 'Dr Blair. That's the first I've seen of him today.'

Over a green scrubsuit Dr Blair wore a clear plastic apron that had smears of blood on the front. Lisa looked at him expectantly as the two groups converged, waiting for him to acknowledge her presence. He looked tense and absorbed, talking rapidly to his two colleagues.

Dr Blair's eyes skated over the trio of nurses, giving no indication that their presence had actually registered with him. His expression did not change. Then they were gone.

Lisa felt a sharp, irrational disappointment as she hurried to keep up with her head nurse. That was probably how things were going to be from now on. She and Dr Blair would be colleagues, nothing more.

At two o'clock in the afternoon Lisa prepared to go off duty, which was the end of her designated work shift as a part-time nurse. All the time she had been at work part of her mind had been on Emma Kate. She knew that once the orientation period was over all her attention would have to be on the job. Clearly, it was going to be very demanding—she was actually looking forward to rising to the challenge.

She had a shower in the nurses' change-room, before putting on her outdoor clothing and walking out. A street-car would take her very close to home, even though it was a slow journey. She had cancelled the insurance on her car, not being able to afford to run it. 'I don't really miss it,' she said to herself as she walked out into the almost balmy air of early spring. After the winter almost anything would seem balmy, she mused.

Throughout that busy morning she and Marcus Blair had not said one word to each other.

'She's getting a bit cranky.' Mrs Stanton greeted Lisa with those words as she let herself into her flat from the back garden where she had her own private entrance. 'I held off giving her the bottle for her feed because I knew you would want to feed her yourself when you came in.'

Lisa's mother was holding Emma in her arms with the baby's head up against her shoulder, jiggling her up and down. 'Do you think it's going to work this way, Lisa—you trying to continue with the breast-feeding?'

Flinging her raincoat and bag onto a chair, Lisa reached for her baby. 'I've missed her so much.' She kissed the plump cheek that was nearest to her. 'Thanks, Mum. I'm going to try to keep my own milk going as long as possible. I know it won't be easy—my breasts feel pretty engorged right now. All through the morning I was worried that I would be leaking milk through my uniform.' She exchanged commiserating smiles with her mother.

'She's just working up to a temper,' her mother cautioned. 'You know, she gets red in the face, and then she lets out a yell when she's really mad.'

'Yes.' Lisa laughed. 'I'll feed her right away.'

'All right. I'll take myself off. I've got some phone calls to make. All in all, she's been pretty good—slept a lot of the time.'

'Have you been good, eh?' Lisa crooned to her baby as she sat in a comfortable chair and prepared to feed her. Emma Kate gave her that gummy, adoring smile that she reserved just for her. Somehow it made everything worthwhile.

As the baby sucked vigorously Lisa's thoughts turned unwillingly to Richard. On and off, during the last three months, she had thought of contacting him and telling him that he had a daughter. During her pregnancy she had called his number four times. It had not been easy to get up the courage to do so. Always a woman had answered so she had hung up without uttering a word. Pride had prevented her from calling again. . .or from telling Marcus Blair that she had tried. Now she knew that Richard wouldn't give a damn.

There was an ache of longing in her heart when she thought of some of the good times they had shared. Being back in University Hospital had brought back to her, poignantly, all that had taken place between them, all the times they had worked together.

Lisa looked over at the telephone, standing on a small side table next to her comfortable old sofa. It would be so easy to dial his number, the number he had given her when he had left in case there were any messages for him. Then she knew that she would not do it, not again. Maybe it was pride—she wasn't sure what it was. She bit her lower lip hard. 'Don't cry,' she told herself sternly as she felt the sting of tears in her eyes, 'for God's sake, don't cry.'

At times like this, when she held her daughter, she thought that he ought to know—ought to be with them. Sometimes she longed for his arms around her—even though she knew he was a taker, not a giver.

'I'm beginning to think that you're the best thing that ever happened to me,' Lisa whispered to Emma Kate. 'We love each other, no holds barred.'

The rest of the week went by very quickly, with both Lisa and Diane working in the reception area with the two other permanent staff nurses who worked there. They were called triage nurses, which meant the sorting and classification of all patients who came into the emergency department. Behind privacy screens they examined patients to determine their priority. Stretcher cases had a separate entrance and triage nurse. For now, both Lisa and Diane were in the ambulatory patient section.

'Hullo, Anne,' Lisa greeted Diane on the Friday morning as she had greeted her on the other mornings, making a joke out of their enforced change of name.

'Hullo, Liz,' Diane replied, grinning. They had agreed to use their own names only when no patients were within earshot.

'Well, we've almost made it through one week,' Lisa said with satisfaction. 'Only two more weeks of this to go, then they'll throw us into the deep end and expect us to swim on our own.'

'I don't suppose we'll see anything much that we haven't seen before,' Diane said philosophically. 'After all, anatomy and physiology doesn't change. And we know the world's a violent place. Right?'

'Right.'

They waited expectantly together in the reception area, ready for anything that the ambulances might disgorge at the entrance or anything else. Already there were a number of people in the ambulatory area waiting room who had been categorized in order of priority. The more junior doctors in the department were working their way through them, together with the residents-in-training.

'Hi, what's next?' Dr Nathan Hanks, a senior resident, came into the triage unit and took the next patient card that the nurses had ready in a file of patients to be seen.

'There's a young guy in cubicle one,' Lisa said, intercepting him, 'that I'm worried about. He just came in. Could you see him first?'

'Sure, Lisa,' he said good-humouredly. 'Anything a former OR nurse says has to be believed. Lead me to him, but fill me in first.'

'Superficially, it doesn't appear to be much,' Lisa said, 'but with all the necrotizing fasciitis we've been hearing about in the last few weeks I don't feel happy about him.'

'What's he got?'

'A swelling on one side of his face, right over the cheek area, extending down to the jaw line and a bit beyond. And what I don't like is that he's got a faint red line extending down his neck. The funny thing is that he's got no injury, no abrasion, no pimple or anything like that. He's twenty-five years old. I asked him if he cut himself shaving—he said he didn't. It's a bit of a mystery.'

'Hmm. Do you think he's HIV positive?'

'I asked him that,' Lisa replied. 'He said not. He's never been tested because he has no reason to be, so he said.'

'OK. Take me to him.'

All the examination cubicles were full in the ambulatory section of the department, as well as there being a few people in the waiting room. Lisa felt uneasy about the young man she had just described so she had given him top priority for the moment. Dr Hanks followed her out.

If he did indeed have, as she suspected, a streptococcal group A type of infection, which caused haemolytic streptococcal gangrene—otherwise known as necrotizing fasciitis—it was imperative for them to get treatment with antibiotics started immediately. Every moment of delay allowed the deadly, fast-spreading bacteria to gain a hold, probably in some other part of the body. A massive infection could ensue and the patient could be dead within a matter of hours.

Inside the cubicle they found the young patient lying on the examination couch where Lisa had left him a short while before.

'Hi, Mr Reese, I'm Dr Hanks. Tell me how long you've had this swelling on your face.' Dr Hanks put on a pair of surgical rubber gloves and began to palpate the man's cheek, which was definitely swollen. His fingers rippled over it so they could clearly see that a considerable amount of fluid had gathered under the skin. There was only a small area of redness.

'Well. . .' the young man cleared his throat nervously, obviously worried, yet trying to hide the fact '. . .I first noticed it yesterday morning. . .didn't think much of it. Then today it was worse. When the swelling got down to the jaw line I was worried—thought I'd better come in here.'

'His temperature isn't elevated,' Lisa offered.

'You say you didn't nick yourself while shaving?' Dr Hanks said.

'No.'

'Is there any other way that the skin could have been broken? I don't see any evidence that the skin has been broken—there's just this small red area.'

'No, I didn't have anything on my face. That's why it's so odd,' Ed Reese said. 'It's not really painful, just feels a bit tight.'

'How do you feel generally?'

'I feel all right. Just a bit tired, that's all.'

'It could have started with an infected hair follicle,' Dr Hanks murmured, 'Anyway, you sure did the right thing in coming in here. There's an infection there, even if we can't see an obvious source. . .and I don't like the look of that red line running down your neck. That means the infection is spreading. I want to examine you and ask you some questions, then we'll get you started on antibiotics.'

'Thanks, Doctor.' Ed Reese sounded relieved.

'Um, Liz,' Dr Hanks said, just remembering her 'official' name in time. 'Would you get Dr Blair to take a look at this? I'd like his opinion before I start treatment. And we'd better take Mr Reese's temperature again—it could have changed in the last few minutes, although he doesn't look as though he's got a fever yet. Get Dr Blair first.'

As Lisa hurried out she realized that this would actually be the first time she would speak to Marcus Blair since she had started work in the department. He had actually come face to face with her two days ago and had acknowledged her presence with a smile. Usually he worked on the other side of the department where the serious emergency and stretcher cases came in, only coming over to the ambulatory side when he was needed for a consultation.

Lisa straightened her uniform self-consciously and

tucked back some of her hair, which had escaped from the light, disposable paper hat that she wore, as she went in search of Dr Blair. She found that she wanted an excuse for interaction with him, and her heart lifted at the prospect of actually talking to him, however briefly.

'Is Dr Blair in here?' Lisa asked a nurse in one of the operating and resuscitation rooms, having looked in his office and elsewhere for him without success.

'What do you want him for?' the nurse asked sharply, blocking her entry.

'Dr Hanks wants him in cubicle one on the other side for a consultation,' Lisa explained.

'Don't just come barging in here,' the other nurse complained. 'This is an operating room, you know. I'll give Dr Blair the message.

'Thank you,' Lisa said, taken aback by the other woman's unfriendly attitude. She was the first bad-tempered staff member Lisa had encountered so far.

'Is that you, Lisa?' the deep voice of Dr Blair enquired from inside the room so that the other nurse was forced to open the door wider. Then Marcus Blair appeared, wiping his hands on a towel. A disposable surgical mask hung around his neck. He was bare-headed, his dark hair dishevelled, and he looked tired. 'Dr Hanks wants me?'

'Yes, if you're free,' Lisa said apologetically, suffering the glower of the other nurse. Perhaps she was one of those nurses, Lisa mused, who considered certain doctors her own property, or maybe just one doctor in particular. They were a fairly common breed, usually dedicated career nurses who had not found time to find a husband or a boyfriend.

'I am free,' Dr Blair said rather pointedly, subtly putting the obtuse nurse in her place. 'I'll find the time. And how are you these days, Miss Stanton?'

'I'm fine, thank you,' Lisa said hastily, while she registered from the other woman's ID badge that her name was Marie, and she made a silent vow to avoid Marie as much as possible in the future.

As they walked back together to cubicle one Marcus asked her how she liked the department so far.

'I like it,' she said, giving him a small, hesitant smile. Then she went in ahead of him.

'Hi, Marcus. Thanks for coming,' Dr Hanks said. 'I wanted you to take a look at this in case it could be staphylococcus A. I haven't given him anything yet.'

As the patient was examined once again, with Marcus palpating the swelling carefully and asking more questions, Lisa went to fetch sterile IV tubing from a supply kept just outside the cubicle, together with a small bag of intravenous saline and an array of broad-spectrum antibiotics. She suspected that the patient, whatever the immediate diagnosis, would need intravenous antibiotics.

Marcus looked at her when she came back with the equipment. 'Like the nurse says,' he remarked, looking at what she had in her hands, a slight smile on his face, 'give an IV bolus of cloxacillin. Run it in slowly with the fluid. That was what you were going to do anyway, wasn't it, Dr Hanks?'

'Yeah.' Nathan Hanks grinned. 'What about incising this? Looks like there might be a little pus under this red part. The rest is just serous fluid, I guess.'

'We won't incise it until he's had the cloxacillin and it's had a chance to keep the infection in check,' Marcus said. 'Give him oral cloxacillin to take home as well, then we'll do it tomorrow. Mr Reese,' he addressed the patient, 'could you come back here tomorrow morning fairly early? We'd like to make a tiny cut just here—let out any pus that might be there and take a swab for a lab culture, even though the drugs may have killed off most of the bacteria by then. This could be something serious so it's not something you can neglect.'

'Yeah, I can come back,' Ed Rees agreed. 'Have I. . . have I got flesh-eating disease?' His voice was high-pitched with anxiety.

Marcus hesitated. 'This could be caused by the same bacteria that cause that disease, which is why we're going to treat it aggressively,' he said carefully. 'If you had the disease you wouldn't be feeling very well. However, you did the right thing by coming to us early so that we can nip this thing in the bud.'

'Right.'

'And we won't know if it's the same bacteria until we take a swab tomorrow and wait a day or two for the results,' Marcus continued, speaking reassuringly. 'The intravenous antibiotics we're going to give you will zap anything quite nicely. Usually, with so-called flesh-eating disease, there's a definite abrasion or cut in the skin through which the organisms can gain entry.'

'I'm a bit run down—working a lot lately,' Ed Reese said.

'That could be a factor,' Marcus said. 'Your natural defences are lowered. Make sure you continue the antibiotics at home for ten days. Usually we like to take a swab for culture before we give any antibiotics, but in this case we want to get started with them and then we'll see you tomorrow.'

As Dr Hanks prepared to insert the intravenous line Dr Blair drew Lisa out of the cubicle with him when he left. 'It's a good idea to scare them a bit,' he said, 'otherwise they never come back, or they never finish the full course of antibiotics. Anyway, I guess you know that, don't you, Lisa? Being an experienced nurse.'

'Yes,' she said. They were standing close in a busy

corridor. 'Well, thank you. I must get back in there to help Dr Hanks.'

'Would you go with him to the pharmacy—make sure he's got the oral drugs? I'm pretty sure he'll get them but I just want to make sure.' Marcus said.

'Yes.' Lisa took off her cap that made her scalp itch and ran her fingers unconsciously through her thick, shiny hair, thinking about Ed Reese. Marcus looked at her movements, his eyes travelling slowly from her hair to her mouth, as though he was familiarizing himself with each feature of her face. All at once there was an almost unbearable awareness between them, and again Lisa felt her throat constricting with tension.

Then he looked at her breast, where the fabric of her uniform top was pulled taut by her uplifted arm. Slowly Lisa lowered her arm to her side, feeling as though she could not get her breath. For a few seconds it felt as though they were the only two people in the bustling corridor. Something strange was happening to her. Images of Richard were very gradually being replaced by images of Marcus Blair—and that frightened her. It would not do for her to get a schoolgirl crush on him. There was no way that she wanted a repeat performance. Yet this was different. . .

His eyes locked with hers for a moment, intensely searching, before he looked away down the corridor where a stretcher had come through the centre doors of the department. When he looked at her again his gaze was distant, somehow impersonal. 'Please make sure,' he said stiffly, 'that Mr Reese is given an appointment card to be back here at a very specific time. I want him here at 8 a.m. sharp. Dr Hanks is on duty over the weekend—he'll do it. Make a note of that.'

Lisa moistened her dry lips, staring at him as though mesmerized. 'I'll do that,' she said.

Then he was gone, striding away from her—weaving his way through the hurrying staff and patients. Lisa stared after him, feeling dazed, her eyes fixed on his dark hair until he was out of sight. Something had happened between them—she wasn't sure what. During that week she had experienced the odd feeling that he had been avoiding her. She had told herself that she didn't figure so highly in his scheme of things that he would bother to avoid her. He was much too straightforward for that, wasn't he? And his life was hectic.

Back in the cubicle she prepared the antibiotic to go into the small bag of intravenous fluid that Nathan Hanks had up and running.

'You're going to have to lie here for a while, Mr Reese,' Dr Hanks said. 'We'll run this in slowly. Keep an eye on him, Liz.'

Back at the triage station a little later Lisa went through the cards of the waiting patients. All the cubicles were full. The next patient to be seen was a boy with a dog bite to his arm. That would have to be cleaned up, irrigated and a dressing put on. His mother had said that he was up to date with his tetanus immunization, but they would have to check it.

They had had children with burns, patients with sore throats, coughs, colds, chest pains, difficulty with breathing, abrasions, lacerations, foreign bodies inhaled or swallowed, bruises, concussions, dislocated shoulders, earache, stomach aches, backache, sprains and foreign bodies in eyes. Anything they couldn't deal with had been sent round to the section for serious cases—there had been a patient who had vomited blood, someone who had taken a lot of pills in order to commit suicide but was still walking—those had been transferred.

'What can I do next?' A young woman intern came into the triage station.

'Well, there's that woman with pelvic pain and an elevated temperature,' Lisa said. 'We're waiting for the senior gynae resident to see her. He should be here any minute. Otherwise it's the boy with the dog bite.'

'I guess she's got pelvic inflammatory disease,' the intern said, looking at the preliminary card. 'Probably venereal in nature, with half a dozen other things as well, and herpes thrown in. Those things are the devil to treat. They're resistant to all sorts of antibiotics.'

'Maybe you should settle for the dog bite,' Lisa said.

Just as she went out to check the waiting room a familiar voice hailed her. 'Hi. . . Mrs Stanton. Lisa, isn't it?'

It was Dr Rick Kates, the obstetrics and gynae resident, whom she had not seen since she had come in herself as a patient.

'Remember me?' he said, grinning.

'How could I ever forget you?' Lisa smiled.

'How are you and the baby?'

'We're both good.'

'Say. . .' He frowned. 'Aren't you married to Marcus Blair? He was with you that night.'

Looking around her hastily—not wanting to have her personal affairs aired in public—Lisa saw that there were several people in the waiting room who appeared to be listening to the hasty verbal exchange. 'Shh!' she said. 'Not so loud, Dr Kates.'

She took his arm and marched him towards the cubicle containing the woman with pelvic pain. 'We've been waiting for you,' she said. 'No, I am not married to Marcus Blair. It was just a subterfuge because he happened to be around when I needed someone. It's a long story.'

'OK.' Dr Kates grinned. 'I won't press you for details. Pity he's not married to you. I reckon that guy needs a wife.'

'Why?'

'Working in this place, you need some one to go home to.'

'Now, about this patient, Dr Kates. She's a probable pelvic inflammatory disease. There's a gynae examination tray in the cubicle. I'll be with you in a couple of minutes when you want to examine her.'

With that, she left him and went back to Ed Reese to check on the intravenous line to make sure it was still dripping and at the required rate. She felt breathless and a little irritated, wishing that Dr Kates hadn't recognized her, although she didn't doubt that he would say no more about it to her or anyone else.

The rest of her shift went by in a flurry of activity, with no time for a break. It was half past two when she finally hurried out of the main doors to go home, having made a hasty telephone call to her mother to say that she was on her way.

Preoccupied with thoughts of Emma Kate, she didn't at first see the woman who had stepped into her path on the sidewalk outside the emergency department until she came face to face with her.

'Are you Lisa Stanton?' the woman said, as Lisa stopped abruptly in front of her to avoid a collision.

'Yes, I am,' she said immediately, without thinking. Then the words of Sadie Drummond came to her about never giving out your real name, and she could have kicked herself.

The woman appeared to be in her thirties, although she looked a little older. Her face was tired, thin and heavily made-up, and the word 'raddled' came to Lisa's mind as she looked at her at close quarters, before stepping back. She had long, blonde dyed hair that might have looked appropriate on a teenager, but looked somewhat bizarre on this woman. She was quite attractive, with large, pale eyes.

'Are you married to Marcus Blair?' the woman said.

Surprised, Lisa could only stare for a few moments. Then the recollection of where she had seen the woman before came to her. The woman had been sitting in the waiting room at the time she and Dr Rick Kates had exchanged words. And another thing... This woman hadn't registered at the front desk—Lisa was pretty sure of that. Yet she had been sitting in the waiting room. Perhaps she had accompanied a patient.

'Who are you?' she said slowly, more careful this time. 'Why do you want to know that?'

'Just answer the question,' the woman snarled, an expression of dislike on her face.

'I don't know you,' Lisa said. 'Why are you questioning me?'

'Marcus Blair's in love with me,' the woman said, 'and it's mutual. I come here to be near him while he's working.'

Lisa assessed the woman, who wore a short metal-coloured raincoat, black stockings and high-heeled shoes—an outfit too flimsy for the cool weather. She carried a garishly coloured handbag.

The feeling of disquiet deepened as Lisa's professional instincts told her that something very odd was going on and that she had to be careful. Swallowing an apprehensive lump in her throat, she lifted her head up and stared at the woman full in the face.

'I see,' she said, keeping her voice without inflection.

'No, you don't see, you silly bitch!' the other woman said, her voice rising. 'He's mine! I want to know what the hell you think you're playing at with him.'

'I'm not playing at anything,' Lisa said calmly, her voice belying her inner apprehension. The woman's words were like an unexpected slap in the face. 'Dr Blair and I are colleagues, nothing more. No, I am not married to him. And if, for some strange reason, you are threatening me I'd like you to know that I have a personal alarm right here in my pocket. If you don't explain yourself I intend to set it off. This place is swarming with security people. I suggest you explain yourself.'

'I'm just warning you to stay away from him,' the woman said. 'He's mine. . .and he always will be. He loves me.' She came closer to Lisa who stood her ground, trying not to flinch. 'What did that guy mean about a baby? You have a baby?'

'Yes, I do.' Lisa thought she could see what the woman was getting at. 'It is not Marcus Blair's baby.'

'It had better not be.'

'I suggest that we both go into the emergency department and talk to Marcus,' Lisa said decisively, calling the woman's bluff. 'I'm sure he'll be happy to sort this out for you.'

Perhaps this woman needed a psychiatrist, Lisa thought frantically. At the same time, she was curious to find out whether she was actually known to Marcus.

An odd expression came over the woman's face, a cunning knowingness mingled with reluctance. Feeling on safer ground now, Lisa waited.

'You suggest nothing,' the woman said, after a hesitation. 'I'm calling the shots here. Marcus is busy right now, I know that.'

'In that case, I'll go to see him myself, 'Lisa said decisively. 'Perhaps you have a message for him? If you tell me your name I'll give it to him.'

'Wouldn't you just like to know my name?' The woman laughed, her mouth twisted in a derisive grimace. There was a look of hatred in her eyes. 'You think you're so smart because you're a nurse, working with Marcus. So you've got some sort of alarm in your pocket?' Again she laughed. 'Well, I've got a knife in mine, you smarmy bitch, and another one in my bag.'

While the woman had been talking an ambulance had pulled up at the entrance, bringing with it the ambulance attendants. With relief, Lisa saw them unload two patients on stretchers who, judging by their appearance, had been in a road-traffic accident. They both had blood-soaked dressings on head wounds and surgical collars around their necks for support.

'I'm going in to talk to Dr Blair,' Lisa said, taking advantage of the protective presence of the other personnel. 'If I see you in this department again I'll report you immediately to the security staff.'

Turning on her heel, she walked quickly back the way she had come, not looking behind her. She felt physically and emotionally winded by the encounter.

One of the stretchers was in front of her, one behind. With any luck, she could get to speak to Marcus for a few minutes before all hell broke loose in there. In truth, she was more shaken up than she would care to admit—for a number of reasons. Not least of her concerns was why Marcus would be mixed up with such a woman, who looked like a prostitute—if, indeed, he even knew her.

She did not doubt that the woman was mentally ill. What was frightening was that she might have singled her, Lisa, out for future unwanted attention. Whether she had had a knife in her pocket or not, any such threats had to be taken seriously.

As she walked swiftly and purposefully down the corridor leading to the resuscitation area of the department she saw Marcus walking quickly in her direction to meet the first stretcher, together with the surgical resident and the surgical intern. Then she knew that there was no way she could distract his attention now, let alone talk to him in this emergency.

Flattening herself against a wall to let both stretchers pass, she made a decision to call Marcus from home later in the day. For now, she would just take care to avoid that woman again. She would leave the hospital by a different exit and take a taxi home. If she saw the woman at the hospital again she would report it all to the security people, as she had said.

It was a good thing that she knew the hospital so well that she could walk inside the building to get to an exit on a different street, where she knew there were generally one or two taxis waiting.

CHAPTER FIVE

'SORRY I'm a bit late, Mum.' She greeted her mother with the usual hug and kiss. 'It's been a really hectic day—what you could call crazy.' If only her mother knew!

'Are you all right?' Mrs Stanton asked anxiously, sensing the irony in her words.

'I'm fine, Mum,' she said, and meant it. 'After Ethiopia and Somalia, there isn't much I can't deal with in the wilds of Gresham.'

By the time Lisa had checked on Emma Kate, made herself a mug of coffee and drunk half of it she had come to several decisions. She went to the telephone and punched in a hospital number.

'Locating.' A brisk voice answered after two rings.

'I'm trying to locate Dr Peter Johanson,' she said, 'the senior psychiatric resident.' As she gave her name and number she felt something of a weight being lifted from her shoulders.

Waiting for him to call back, she put on a warm jacket and went out into the garden which was brown and soggy after the long winter months yet with definite signs of spring.

In the last year life had changed irrevocably, she mused. Nothing would ever be the same for her. No more trips to Africa—in case she came back with a deadly disease, or didn't come back at all. Would she ever marry? Would she get over her residual feelings for Richard and be able to find someone else to love who would love her as much in return? At the moment she felt flat, wrung out, drained.

When the phone rang she ran in to snatch up the receiver.

'Peter Johanson here,' a familiar voice said. 'Hullo, Lisa. How are you?'

In short order, she poured out the story to him. 'I want your professional opinion, Peter. Give me some ideas on how I should deal with this. . .please.'

Peter was known to her because he had been in the same class as Richard at medical school. They had met socially, as well as having had many conversations over lunch in the hospital cafeteria. He was discreet, sensible, reliable.

'Well, first of all, I think you should talk to Marcus Blair. I haven't met him myself so he's an unknown quantity—see if he knows this woman,' he said. 'Then you should definitely go to hospital security and give them a description of her. Never take any chances, Lisa. Think of the worst-case scenario, assume that it could take place and then take precautions before something could happen. If you should encounter her again don't try to reason with her because you won't be able to. These people have their own brand of logic which, believe me, is out of sync with everybody else's.'

'What do you think the problem is?'

'She's probably one of those obsessive women—an "erotomanic", as they're known to the police—who live in a fantasy world and who believe certain men to be in love with them, or that those men have fathered their children when the guys themselves don't even know the woman in many cases,' Peter explained. 'You know, like the groupies who follow rock stars around the country. Maybe this woman was a patient of Dr Blair's at one time.'

'She was very threatening,' Lisa said. 'Could she actually be dangerous?'

'Usually such women are not dangerous, in my experience—not like the guys who stalk women,' Peter Johanson said thoughtfully. 'But there's always the exception to the rule, Lisa. Never take any chances. Something could trigger her, and she could go over the top and get violent. For some reason, she seems to be jealous of you—maybe because she overheard that brief conversation.'

'Yes, I think that must be it.'

'If she gets fixated on that she could flip. If you knew her name we could check our computers here to see if she's been admitted or had treatment in any psychiatric unit in the city,' he offered.

'She wouldn't give it to me.'

'She could be a psychopath,' he added, as though they were discussing the weather, all in a day's work. 'That could be a whole new ball game. Those people are always looking out for number one. To them, other people are objects to be manipulated. Let me know if you spot her again. If you want me to be involved further I can be.'

Later, when Lisa had fed Emma, cuddled her for a while and put her back to sleep, she dialled Marcus Blair's number, thinking that he might be off duty by then. An answering machine came on after six rings, with his voice asking any caller to leave a message. Slowly she hung up, not wanting to leave a message.

After a leisurely, relaxing bath she put on a pair of comfortable black leggings and a large, loose red sweater that came down over her hips. As she used the blow-dryer on her damp hair she planned the remainder of the day. Somehow she would get through the inevitable chores that having a baby entailed, then she might even have time to take Emma Kate for a ride in her padded stroller now that the snow was gone.

The doorbell rang just as she was finishing cooking her supper and Emma was kicking and gurgling on the floor of a small playpen that Lisa had set up in her sitting room.

'Now who could that be?' She spoke aloud, pushing a hand through her dishevelled hair, mindful that she wore no make-up and her face was flushed from the heat of the stove. Only her closest friends came round to the side door of the house that was her personal entrance, and they usually called before they came.

She saw the outline of a man through the frosted glass panel in the door. Could it be Richard? Sick with anticipation, she paused and bit her lip, reluctant to open the door. Uppermost was the swift knowledge that she didn't want to see him. Such a revelation told her something she had been hoping for—that she was getting over him. Could he somehow have found out that she had a baby? Slowly she inched the door open on its safety chain.

'Hullo, Lisa,' a deep voice greeted her. 'Forgive me for not calling first. I decided to just come personally.'

'Um. . .Marcus. . .Dr Blair,' she found herself stammering. 'Just a moment. . .' Clumsily she eased off the chain, asking herself frantically why he would be there. Perhaps he wanted to see Emma.

'Please come in,' she said, standing back to admit him. He wore a warm overcoat and looked very masculine, almost imposing, at the entrance to her tiny flat. His presence made her feel suddenly very womanly, making her realize how much she had longed for mature male company throughout her pregnancy and beyond.

'Call me Marcus,' he said, aware that she was flustered. 'I came because your number was on the call-display unit on my telephone.'

'Oh. . .'

'I wondered why you hadn't left a message. May I take my coat off?' His dark, observant gaze ran over her quickly.

'Oh, yes. . .please do.' She hovered while he slipped out of his coat. Underneath it he wore casual grey trousers and a grey sweater over an open-necked shirt. Lisa found that she could not take her eyes off him for those first few moments.

'I. . .um. . .didn't leave a message because I had something to discuss with you,' she said, as she draped his coat over the stair rail leading up to the second floor. 'I decided that I didn't want to leave all that on a machine.'

'All that?' he queried.

Lisa paused, wondering how to broach the subject of the crazy woman. That was how she was now thinking of her more than ever, not wanting to exaggerate the implications of it all.

'Yes. I didn't expect you to come here. You must be tired.'

They were standing very close in the hallway and he was looking at her curiously, astutely, his eyebrows slightly raised. There was concern in that glance so that all at once Lisa knew it would be a relief to pour it out to him. Also, it was imperative that she know what connection, if any, he had with that woman. . .

Just then the chortling of the baby in the next room intruded on their conversation. 'Well, are you going to let me see Emma?' Marcus said softly. 'I've been looking forward to it.' The slight stiffness that she had detected in his manner earlier that day had been replaced, it seemed to her, by a certain polite formality.

'That's nice, since she doesn't have a father,' Lisa found herself saying without thinking, recognizing the tinge of bitterness in her own voice.

'You could remedy that, perhaps,' Marcus said quietly. 'She *does* have a father.'

Lisa felt her face become stiff, her pleasure at seeing him erased. 'No, I couldn't, Dr Blair,' she blurted. 'You don't know the details. It's none of your business really, is it?'

They faced each other in stunned silence. Marcus's face was impassive, his mouth set in a stern line.

'You're right,' he said at last, his voice neutral. 'It is none of my business. I just happen to believe that a child needs a father.'

'You think I don't?' she demanded quietly, her voice breaking. 'You think that I don't agonize over it every day of my life?' Things seemed to be going wrong between them, and quite suddenly Lisa found that she wanted to weep. Why on earth had she said that? It was ridiculous that they should be almost quarrelling when he had been in her house for about three minutes.

'I don't know what you think, Lisa,' he said, some of his tiredness showing through as he regarded her thoughtfully. 'I hope you'll tell me. . .some time, if not now.'

Although Lisa's throat felt tight with tension she managed to get the words out. 'I've decided that an unhappy mother is worse for a child than no father,' she said, putting into words, really for the first time, what had been gradually formulating in her mind over the last months. 'Wondering where he is all the time, who he's with. . . and why. He would be inadequate in the role. He's not just some lovable guy who can't wait to be a father.'

'Hmm. . . I hope you'll let me see her, anyway.'

'She's in the sitting room,' Lisa said bluntly after several awkward moments, gesturing towards the room.

At the sight of a strange man Emma immediately lapsed into silence and stopped waving her arms and legs as she lay on her back in the centre of the playpen. Her large, luminous blue eyes moved from Marcus's face to Lisa's and back again. Her mass of fine, dark auburn hair contrasted well with her creamy skin that was glowing with health.

With clenched hands, Lisa stood back a little while the

man with her, who was beginning to feel like a stranger to her, looked down at her child.

'She's lovely,' he said quietly, the words bringing stinging tears to Lisa's eyes. Hastily she blinked several times. She hadn't realized that her emotions were so close to the surface, that she could blow up so easily—she would have to watch that. The last thing she wanted was for him to feel sorry for her, especially when she didn't feel sorry for herself. . .just lonely right now. She would get over it.

Emma wore a pale yellow romper suit and looked utterly adorable.

'Hi, there,' Marcus murmured, looking down at the baby. Lisa found her eyes drawn to his face. There was an intentness, a wistfulness, in his expression that made her feel intuitively, in spite of her anger with him, that he longed for children.

'May I pick her up?' he said.

'Yes.'

As he bent to pick up the child Lisa quietly watched them. At close quarters, as he held her in his arms, Emma also sized up the man sombrely, her eyes roving over his face. The action had the effect of lightening the mood between the two adults.

'Babies don't give their affections lightly to strangers.' Lisa smiled slightly. This should be Emma's father holding her now.

'Very sensible,' he murmured, tenderness in his voice. 'A very good survival tactic.' He looked even bigger and more masculine, holding the tiny scrap of humanity in his arms. 'Perhaps,' he added, 'adults should be more careful in that regard. Hmm?'

The look he gave her was candid, a cynical twist on his sensual mouth contrasting with the tenderness with which he held her baby.

'Are you alluding to me?' she asked. Anger mingled

with a bitter sense of loss for the empathy he had displayed to her when she had been bleeding in the emergency department.

'To both of us,' he said enigmatically. In his glance there seemed to be many unspoken questions that at the moment she dared not interpret. 'Here. . . I think she wants you now. A baby is such a positive thing. Everything else seems trivial by comparison.'

As he handed over Emma her hand touched his, the contact like a touch of fire. She knew that she longed for male company, at the same time realizing that the experience of childbirth, of being a mother, had left her very sober in spirits, almost cynical. Never again would she be a push-over for a man and let her emotional and physical needs rule her head. Anyway, she didn't know how to deal with the very attractive, sophisticated Dr Marcus Blair—even if he were not out of bounds for her.

Was he judging her? Perhaps testing her capabilities as a mother? It was difficult not to get defensive at times when you were a single mother—not to assume that the world was judging you.

'She's just about ready to go to sleep, I think,' Lisa said, wanting to distance herself from him as she left the room.

'I hope I haven't interrupted anything, Lisa,' he said smoothly when she came back, as he stood casually in the centre of the room with his hands in the pockets of his trousers.

There was tension in the room. She wasn't sure whether it emanated from her alone. 'I called you because a woman threatened me today as I was leaving the hospital to come home.' She plunged right into the story. 'She said she knew you, that she. . .that she was in love with you, that you loved her and that I was to stay away from you. . .or something like that.' Then she added, in an attempt at humour, 'I thought it was a bit presumptuous of her, actually.'

Marcus's expression changed to one of rueful cynicism. 'Hell!' he said. 'Bloody hell! It's starting all over again.' With a weary gesture, he passed a hand over his eyes. 'Long blonde hair, dyed? Lots of make-up? Thirty-something?'

'Yes.'

'Who else?' he said tiredly, as though to himself. 'I'm sorry, Lisa, that this has happened to you, more sorry than I can possibly say. We'd better sit down. . . Do you mind? You can tell me what happened, then I can tell my side of it. This is going to take some time. It's a long, convoluted story.'

'You obviously know her,' she commented ruefully, chiding herself for her sense of sharp disappointment. After all, what was Marcus Blair to her or she to him?

'I wish to hell I could say otherwise,' he said harshly. 'She's been the bane of my life over the past four years.'

'Let me make us some coffee,' Lisa offered. 'Or would you prefer a whisky and soda. . .or something?'

In the end they each had a small whisky and soda, followed by coffee. As she prepared the drinks Lisa felt sick with apprehension.

Side by side, one at each end, on the large, comfortable old sofa in her sitting room they sipped their drinks while she told him what had happened that afternoon.

'Do you want to hear the whole story?' Marcus asked. 'I won't bore you with it if you'd rather not.'

'Tell me, please. I don't even know her name—she wouldn't give it to me.' At close quarters she observed him. . .and wished they could talk about something else.

'Her name's Charlene Damero. At least, that's the name she goes by. I think it's not her real name,' Marcus said, and leaned back against the sofa with one arm behind his head and the other holding his glass, his long legs stretched out.

'I'll get through it as quickly as I can. Four years ago I was working in an emergency department here in Gresham. Ms Damero came in as a patient one evening, complaining of severe pain in her breasts. She'd had an operation on her breasts shortly before that, a breast augmentation with implants—the saline variety, not the silicone—purely cosmetic. It's quite common, as you know, for the breast tissue to form very tight scars around the implants, resulting in hard, very painful breasts.'

'Yes. . .'

'That's what happened to her,' Marcus went on, 'and instead of going back to her plastic surgeon during the day, as she should have done, she came into the emergency department. Because she was in pain we admitted her for observation in the emergency overnight ward.'

'I think I'm beginning to see,' Lisa said, finishing her drink and leaning forward to pour coffee for them both from the pot on the table.

'You've probably guessed it,' he said. 'Fortunately, I was never alone with her. There was always a nurse present, otherwise she might have accused me of sexual harassment when I didn't respond to her in the way that she obviously wanted. Although she was clearly in pain, she was also incredibly provocative. I don't think I'm exaggerating when I say that. It turned out that she had been to every emergency department in the city during the previous week. For some reason, she singled me out for special attention.' He laughed cynically. 'Because I had to touch her breasts in order to examine her, she thought I was attracted to her and—so she said—she fell in love with me. Worse, she thought I reciprocated.'

'Very tricky,' Lisa agreed.

'I disabused her of that idea very quickly. At least, I

tried to. She has a peculiar, convoluted way of thinking that prevents her accepting reality. To cut a long story short, she has plagued my life for the past four years, in spite of all my efforts to avoid her. She hangs around my place of work, finds out somehow where I am. She telephones me and hangs around outside my house. I frequently have to employ security guards to prevent her ringing my doorbell.'

'Surely that kind of harassment is against the law,' Lisa ventured, horrified.

'Oh, yes. I took her to court, got a restraining order. Usually those things are directed against men who harass women.' He smiled crookedly. 'She even spent a month in prison.'

'My God! And it still goes on!'

'The prison put her off for a while, then it started up again as it had done before. She always manages to find out where I am,' he explained tiredly. 'To be honest, I can cope with it, even though it's. . .inconvenient. It's when other people get involved that the craziness of it gets to me. The police know her, of course. She's borderline mentally ill, or a psychopath, but difficult to deal with because she can function in society, can hold down a job, and so on. Our institutions would be overflowing if we were to incarcerate everyone who fell into that category.'

'Yes. I guess you have to wait until they actually commit a crime. What will you do?' Lisa commiserated.

'If she threatens you again, if she takes to hanging around the emergency department, the police will be called. The restraining order is still in effect. My dilemma is that I'm reluctant to have her imprisoned because she'll lose her job. There's no point in taking her to court all the time—she has no money to pay costs or fines.'

'How awful. I can see that it's very difficult.'

'My hope is that she'll fall for some other guy and take

the heat off me. So far, it doesn't seem to be happening.'

'Has she had a lot of other plastic surgery?' Lisa asked, making an educated guess.

'She has,' he confirmed. 'Her eyelids, a nose job, lip augmentation and a chin implant, as well as liposuction of various parts of her body.'

Lisa nodded, and handed him a cup of coffee.

'Thanks. Not that I want to judge her on that—it's her life,' he said. 'If people want to make themselves more attractive that's up to them. What is pathetic is that she thinks those things will transform her in such a way that she will be loved. . .' He paused thoughtfully. 'There's a sadness in all this—a pathos. That's partly why she's so difficult to deal with. However, I don't for one moment underestimate her ability to be vicious, possibly dangerous.'

'No. . .'

'Lisa, you mustn't either. Underestimate her, that is.' Marcus slid his arm along the back of the sofa to touch her on the shoulder to emphasize his point. 'I want you to promise me that you'll let me know every time you see her, or if she telephones you. For God's sake, be careful about who gets your telephone number.'

The brief touch, like a caress, seemed a small gesture of normality in the crazy fantasy world that he was describing.

'Yes, I will. I feel for you, I really do. There must be something else that can be done?' she said, frowning in consternation, her previous annoyance gone. 'My own dilemmas seem mild by comparison. Four years! I can't imagine being harassed by someone for four years!'

'Get tough. That will be the answer. More police, more hospital security, who will take her away. They're used to guys who harass nurses, as well as women who harass doctors.' He turned to look at her. 'I'm sorry you've been drawn into this madness, Lisa,' he apologized again.

'It goes with the territory, I guess,' she mumbled.

'Needless to say, it hasn't been exactly positive for my private life. Not many women are understanding in that regard.' There was wry humour in the small smile he gave her.

'Speaking for myself, I think I'll be able to deal with it,' she said, absurdly conscious of his nearness on the sofa that tended to sag in the middle. 'It's almost laughable, in a weird sort of way.'

'I don't want you to have to deal with it, Lisa. I'll deal with it,' he said decisively, 'Call me the moment she surfaces again, if you see her first. I've no doubt that she will. Promise?'

She was forced to look at him, finding that she was nervous of doing so—nervous of his proximity, of his attractiveness. Heaven forbid that she would resemble that woman in any way and develop a crush on him that could never be assuaged.

'Promise?' he insisted again. 'Because if you don't I may have to put a bodyguard on you until I know what form her harassment is going to take this time.'

She was startled. 'Is that really necessary?'

'I hope it won't be, but I can't pretend that I'm not very concerned. You have your baby to think of, too. I feel responsible for the safety of both of you. On Monday we'll go to the hospital security people. OK?'

When she did not immediately answer, her thoughts preoccupied with the image of the garishly lipsticked mouth of the woman who had threatened her and who had looked at her with apparent hatred, Marcus touched her on the shoulder again. 'Lisa?'

'Yes. I'll be all right, Marcus. I'm not going to do anything to provoke her,' she said quietly, occupied with thoughts of what could happen.

'You could maybe provoke her by merely existing,' he murmured. When their eyes met it seemed to her, from the guarded light in his eyes, that there was a definite added dimension to his words yet he did not follow that up. Their faces were close and, against her will, her glance focused on his well-shaped mouth. He was so different from Richard. Somehow he overwhelmed her, in spite of all her efforts not to feel involved.

For a long time she had felt emotionally dead with everyone except her baby and her own parents. Sitting near to Marcus Blair, she felt herself trembling, tentatively, into a renewed life—the feeling vying incongruously with the subject of their conversation. It was bitter-sweet. Maybe this was the wrong man to reawaken her, if that was actually happening. And how much of it came from gratitude to him? She should be with Emma's father, a small protesting voice reminded her.

'Could I invite you for supper?' she asked, standing up as she felt the gnawings of her own hunger. 'I've cooked it. I was just about to eat when you came.'

'Well. . . Thank you. . .yes. I'm sorry I've delayed you.' Although his hesitation was minimal, Lisa felt it acutely.

'Won't take long,' she said lightly as she went to bring the food from her small kitchen to the table in the sitting room. 'It's just salad, pasta and some cold chicken.'

'Sounds great,' he said.

'Glass of wine?'

'Mmm. . .please.'

When they were seated at opposite sides of the pine table, each with a plate of food and a glass of wine, Lisa decided to take the opportunity to question him. She might never get another such chance. 'How has this woman, Charlene Damero, affected your life? I find it all difficult to imagine.' Really she was probing, wanting to know something more about him.

'She has definitely put off two of my very serious girlfriends, as well as several dozen who fell into a less than serious category,' he said, with a self-deprecating smile.

'You're teasing me,' she said, seeing amusement glinting in his eyes. 'I hope that isn't true.' The mood between them was lightening a little more.

'Women don't like men who take off for Africa at short notice, either. I couldn't impose all that on any woman.' There was self-mockery in his tone, as though daring her to question him further about his intimate life.

'Um. . .no,' she agreed, gratified that he was telling her.

'Some men do, of course. It's very selfish of them,' he mused.

Lisa gave him a tight smile. Richard would fit nicely into that category.

'They hope for the best of both worlds—the best for themselves, that is,' he said. 'They work all the hours God gave, seldom get home and when they do they're about as useless as an electric blanket in a power failure.'

Lisa laughed out loud.

He looked at her levelly across the table. 'Also there's the urge to overwork, to be a sort of superman. One thing I am learning is that no one is indispensable in the workplace in a big city. No one. Some are just better than others, that's all.'

'It's nice to meet a doctor who's got that all figured out,' she said succinctly.

'Now you're teasing me,' he murmured.

'No. . .'

'Where one is indispensable,' he went on more soberly, his eyes boring into hers and holding her attention, 'is in one's relationships, in one's role as a lover, a spouse, a close friend—a parent, especially. Wouldn't you agree?'

'Yes. . .' They both seemed to be enclosed in a circle of awareness, held by his intensity.

'A baby, a little kid, needs to be with someone who loves him or her—they don't care how much money you make in a year.'

Lisa bit her lower lip, deciding not to comment—trying not to read judgement of her into his words. Clearly, he did not approve of young women who tried to bring up babies on their own.

'Excuse me.' Lisa got up to bring in a fruit salad she had made, then escaped again to make coffee.

In no time at all he was ready to leave.

'That was a great meal, Lisa. I appreciate it very much,' he said as they stood in the hallway and he put on his coat.

'It was great to have your company,' she said. 'You've made me realize how lonely I get sometimes, in spite of having the most wonderful parents in the world.' That was the understatement of the decade, she thought as she opened the door.

'No hard feelings?' he said.

'No. . .' That wasn't entirely true.

'I'll speak to the security people tonight. I'll talk to you on Monday,' he said.

'Thank you. That's a relief.'

As he was leaving he turned to her in the open doorway. For a heart-stopping moment she thought he was going to kiss her—and she knew that she wanted him to. 'Don't be lonely, Lisa,' he said softly. 'See you next week. Goodbye.'

'Goodbye.'

Lisa watched him walk round the side of the house, feeling a sharp sense of loss as he disappeared. Somehow she knew that he would never risk getting seriously involved with a woman while he had a crazy ex-patient pursuing him. What a waste, what a terrible waste.

CHAPTER SIX

'HELLO, Mr Reese.' Lisa halted in the reception area of the emergency department as Ed Reese came through the entrance doors on Monday morning. 'How are you?'

'Much better, thanks.' Ed Reese gave a small smile of satisfaction. 'I came in on Saturday morning to have the thing cut to let out some of the fluid. I've just come back today to see Dr Hanks for a check-up.'

'Well, the swelling's certainly gone,' Lisa observed, looking at the man's cheek which sported a small Band-aid over the area of the incision. 'Just go into the waiting room and I'll tell Dr Hanks you're here.'

In the triage station Lisa looked up his record on the computer. He was taking the oral cloxacillin, and would be taking it for ten days. Then she went in search of Nathan Hanks among the examination cubicles.

The morning so far had been very much quieter than usual. Like all Emergency Department nurses, she was beginning to distrust such quiet, only thinking of it as the lull before the storm. This week she was to spend time working between the ambulatory section and the stretcher section. If something of a serious nature came in she was to go immediately to help and observe in that area. Sadie Drummond was keeping an eye on her and Diane Crane, otherwise they were left to their own devices until something came in.

'Ah, Dr Hanks,' she hailed him as he went by. 'Mr Reese is here to see you.'

'Great. Just put him into a cubicle, will you? I'll be there in a couple of minutes.'

From then on things went at a steady pace for a while until an ambulance pulled up at the entrance,

'Come on, Lisa.' Diane hurried up to her. 'Here's our first stretcher case of the day. Sadie Drummond wants us over the other side for our orientation.'

'OK.' Lisa punched some information about her last patient into the computer in the triage station, then followed Diane at a brisk pace just as the stretcher was being wheeled through the doors.

'They don't seem to be in a great hurry,' Lisa remarked, looking at the ambulance attendants, 'so I guess it's not an accident case.'

Sadie Drummond met them in the corridor. 'Miss Stanton,' she said, 'I want you to go with Dr Blair to examine this case. He's some one who's known to us. Miss Crane, I want you to help Dr Hanks deal with face lacerations. He'll need to clean up and suture. OK?'

The two nurses nodded, before going off to their assignments. In a treatment room Lisa supervised the transfer of the patient, a middle-aged man, from the stretcher to an examination table.

'This is Mr Carl Ottinger,' the ambulance attendant said to her, handing over a slim folder of notes. 'Sent in by his GP. There's a letter from him in there. Mr Ottinger's been operated on before in this hospital.'

'Thanks.' Lisa took the folder and turned to the patient. 'Hello, Mr Ottinger.'

'Hi,' he said weakly, his voice barely audible. He looked desperately ill, pale and slightly cyanosed, his lips dry and scaled as though he had not had anything to eat or drink for a long time. His eyes were sunken and his face very thin so that his cheekbones jutted out.

Quickly Lisa scanned the GP's letter. Mr Ottinger had metastatic carcinoma, the outcome of an original bowel cancer that had been detected and operated on too late to prevent spread of the disease. Now it looked as though he had intestinal obstruction, possibly at more than one site, as the tumour had spread. Probably it was in his liver as well.

Trying to keep the expression on her face neutral—knowing that the patient was watching her—she felt a wave of sympathy for Mr Ottinger. There would be little anyone could do for him, other than possibly operate to relieve the obstruction temporarily—to give him a colostomy so that at least he could eat and eliminate. A sense of frustration and sadness seemed to pervade the room as she sensed the man's fear and despair.

'Hullo, Lisa. . .or is it Liz?' Dr Blair was there beside her—she hadn't heard his approach.'

She smiled a quick welcome, glad to see him. He looked competent, inspiring confidence, in his green scrubsuit and white lab coat. 'This is Mr Ottinger,' she introduced the patient, handing over the file.

'Good morning, sir.' Marcus acknowledged the patient's presence, before turning to the letter. 'I'm Dr Blair. I see you've been in this hospital before and had surgery here several times.'

'Yes,' the patient said quietly.

'Tell me when this latest problem started.'

'It's been coming on for some time—over the past month,' the patient said, his voice hesitant. 'At first I had difficulty having a bowel movement, then ten days ago I stopped having any bowel movements.' He hesitated, moistening his dry lips with his tongue. 'Three days ago I started to vomit just about everything I ate—not that I had much of an appetite. I forced myself to eat something. In the last two days I've had nothing but water. This morning I started vomiting that as well.'

'You have pain?' Dr Blair asked gently.

'Yes. Pretty awful it is at times.'

'I'd like to examine your abdomen,' Dr Blair said,

easing aside the blanket that covered Mr Ottinger. 'Show me where the pain is most of the time.'

As Marcus palpated the man's abdomen Lisa moved around the room, which was only superficially familiar to her, as she looked for a rectal examination tray, knowing that Marcus would need one. He would most likely want to put down a stomach tube as well to aspirate the stomach contents. She felt like weeping for Mr Ottinger who seemed like an intelligent man, very aware of what was happening to him.

'Thanks, that's great,' Marcus said appreciatively, his tone very professional nonetheless as she brought over both trays. 'I'll want an IV as well as he's pretty dehydrated. And. . .um, Liz, could you call Admitting, find out if we've got any vacant surgical beds, then get on to the senior surgical resident on Dr Claibourne's team, Ted Logan. He may be in the operating room at this time of day. If he is, leave a message for him to come down here as soon as he's free.'

'All right.'

'I'll want to take some blood for a stat haemoglobin,' Marcus continued, talking quietly to her. 'If it's very low, as I suspect it is, I'll consider giving him a blood transfusion to raise it a little so the lab should do a cross-match as well. He'll feel much better if we can do that, as well as get him rehydrated. Then we'll arrange for a scan to find out where the obstruction is.'

It was three quarters of an hour before Dr Ted Logan could get down to see Mr Ottinger and make arrangements to have him admitted. In the meantime, he had been made comfortable with something to relieve his pain and an intravenous line inserted so that he could be given fluid. Marcus had inserted a gastric tube.

'He's got an elevated temperature, Dr Logan,' Lisa said

to him, handing over the file, 'and we've reserved a bed for him, if you will OK it with Admitting.'

'Yes. Can you make the arrangements to get him transferred? Once he's admitted I'll get Jerry Claibourne to see him. Maybe we can operate on him later today—do a colostomy. The sooner the better. He's malnourished, poor devil. I don't think he would stand up to much.'

Lisa sighed. 'No. We're going to give him the two units of blood. We should be getting it from the lab very soon.'

'That's great.'

When Dr Logan had gone she went to find Marcus to make arrangements for the transfer. She found him in the middle of suturing a young man with multiple lacerations.

'I'm going to admit Mr Ottinger, Dr Blair. It's all arranged,' she informed him quietly.

'Good.' He drew her to one side. 'It's important not to write off these patients. I like to go to see them later. Maybe you should, too. He's pretty depressed, to begin with. It's important that we make him feel that something can be done for him, that something *is* actually being done.'

'Yes,' she said.

'Don't transfer him until we have the blood here so we can start him on the first unit. We'll get that haemoglobin level up as quickly as we can.'

'Right. And I'll go to see him when I get off duty,' she said. 'I've informed his son and daughter. He doesn't seem to have a wife.'

'By the way.' He was frowning, speaking in a low voice so that his patient would not hear. 'I've spoken to the security department. If Ms Damero appears here again we are to let them know immediately. Their tactic will be to escort her out instantly, provided she has no legitimate reason for being in here. If she still hangs about on hospital property the police will be called to take her away.'

'That's a relief,' Lisa said feelingly.

'We are to avoid dealing directly with her ourselves. We'll refer her to another staff member.'

They worked together a lot that day, she and Marcus, and for the remainder of the week. Getting to know Marcus Blair as a colleague was proving to be a pleasant and interesting experience, Lisa acknowledged, even though it was very obvious to her that he was deliberately being very professional with her, subtly keeping her at a distance—as though he needed to do it for reasons of his own, as though he disapproved of her somehow, maybe.

Sometimes she would look up quickly to find him watching her with a sombre, unreadable expression, and she would feel a slow heat of confusion coming over her, together with a mental replay of all the scenes preceding the birth of her child which he had shared and which were so vividly etched on her mind.

At the same time, she didn't particularly want to admit her growing attraction to him as a man. The hectic nature of their job made that avoidance relatively easy while she was at work. At home it was a different story, as she found her thoughts turning to him more frequently than to Richard Decker. Somehow Emma Kate seemed to belong more to Marcus than to Richard—and that feeling became stronger as time went by.

Friday dawned warm, unusually so for April, and very windy. By mid-morning they had seen and dealt with a steady flow of patients. At eleven o'clock Sadie Drummond came into the plaster room where Lisa was helping an orthopaedic resident put a plaster of Paris on a fractured leg.

'Miss Stanton,' she said, 'we have five men coming in who fell off a collapsed scaffolding at a building site.

They'll be here in about ten to fifteen minutes. We don't know yet what their injuries are.'

'We're just finishing here,' Lisa said.

'Right! Leave the cleaning up till later.'

The first ambulances, two of them, arrived twelve minutes later. One after the other four stretchers came crashing through the central double doors, accompanied by paramedics. All patients had IV lines running. Two triage nurses were there to meet them. Lisa, who had just handed over her patient with the fractured leg to a more junior nurse, surveyed the front lobby hastily, before going to her new assignment.

'Crushing injury to the chest, head injury, fractured pelvis, probable internal abdominal injuries, fractured right femur, dislocated right shoulder, multiple lacerations to face and hands,' a paramedic stated as he kept moving.

With a quick, assessing glance at the patient the nurse waved them on. 'The last room down there, room three,' she said.

'That's your patient, Miss Stanton,' Sadie Drummond called after Lisa as she hurried to be in the appropriate room before the injured man. 'Stay with Dr Blair. Elsa Graham is the senior nurse there—you'll work with her.' One stretcher followed another in quick succession.

'Help me open these sterile packs,' Elsa Graham said calmly when Lisa joined her in the resuscitation room. 'Although everything might seem chaotic to the casual observer, it's all highly organized here. Nothing's left to chance. We have to be really on the ball. Each member of the trauma resuscitation team has a specific job to do, a routine to follow, as you'll see in a few seconds.'

Within those seconds the two of them had the sterile packs open.

'These trays contain absolutely everything we could

possibly need for now,' Elsa said, deftly and efficiently arranging instruments. 'We resuscitate the patient, then he goes directly to the main operating room. Assuming he doesn't die on us, that is. Bring that bronchoscope set-up over here, Lisa. We have that ready in case the guys have trouble intubating patients, or if there's blood in the lungs.'

As she spoke the other members of the team surged into the room, as though in one body, together with the stretcher holding the groaning patient. Observing him quickly, Lisa could see that his colour wasn't good and that he was gasping painfully for breath as they transferred him to an operating table under powerful lights. Everyone was very calm—there were no heroics.

'Here's the tracheostomy tray,' Elsa Graham said tersely to Lisa, 'in case we have to do a trach on one of them.' If a patient had to be on a respirator for any length of time, or if he needed to be suctioned out so that he could breathe, he would need an opening cut into his throat later.

Elsa and Lisa each put on a long plastic apron and a green surgical gown.

Marcus Blair, as the trauma surgeon and head of the department, was the team leader. There were three highly skilled registered nurses, as well as others, standing by, of whom Lisa and Diane were two. Then there were three other doctors, whom she quickly identified—the residents in anaesthesia, general surgery and orthopaedics. As Elsa had said, each person on the team had a preassigned job, a routine.

Lisa watched with fascination, her adrenalin running high, as this formidable team went to work on their first patient in resuscitation room three. The patient was beyond answering questions, his face grey from loss of blood and his breathing laboured, so the surgical resident questioned the paramedics about his injuries as he prepared to insert a urinary catheter while the anaesthesia resident moved to intubate the patient.

One of the nurses began to insert two more IV lines and the other two nurses began taking equipment from the packs in order to commence procedures. Sadie Drummond began to cut off the patient's clothing.

'Elsa,' Marcus said, 'I'll need bilateral chest tubes, by the look of it, then Dr Logan will start the mini-laparotomy to determine abdominal bleeding. We'll do them simultaneously. He probably has a ruptured spleen and liver. Get the runner to take the blood samples to the lab.'

'Right.'

'Miss Stanton,' Sadie Drummond commanded, 'put on a pair of sterile gloves and help Dr Blair put in those chest tubes. You'll need the underwater seal for those tubes once they're in—they're right here, with the chest pump and the respirator.'

Immediately Lisa began to sort through her tray of sterile instruments.

'The first priority,' Marcus said to Lisa, pulling on a pair of rubber gloves as a nurse tied up his surgical gown at the back, 'is to ensure that the patient can breathe—that he has a supply of oxygen. Thus, we intubate him immediately so that we can help him to breathe by mechanical means if necessary. The paramedics have been giving him oxygen.'

'He's intubated,' the anaesthesia resident confirmed, connecting up his endotracheal tube to the oxygen supply with expert ease.

'If there's blood in the chest cavity, or in the lungs themselves,' Marcus continued, 'we have to get that out very quickly, as you know.'

'I'm ready, Dr Blair,' she said, passing him a sponge-holder loaded with a sponge and a small bowl of iodine solution.

With swift, deft strokes he began to swab the patient's bare chest with the solution. 'The anaesthesia resident takes care of the inside of the lungs while I deal with the chest cavity,' he said. 'Have the scalpel ready. I'll use a trocar first to let out some of the air from the cavity. . . Looks as though he's got several fractured ribs on both sides, probably perforating the lungs. . .so he's got partial collapse of both lungs.'

'Right!' Lisa felt her face growing warm behind the confining surgical mask. In one hand she had a sterile drape ready, then she would pass the scalpel.

'I'm sure I don't need to tell you that we have to let out the accumulated air from the chest cavity so that the lungs can re-inflate,' Marcus said.

As he spoke he worked expertly, first inserting a metal trocar through the chest wall. There was a rush of air out of it. 'I'm going to put the tube though the ninth intercostal space. . .like so. Watch that trocar, Lisa. Block it off as he breathes in. Stand by with the suction. Pass me a tube—quickly. I'll need that silk suture on a straight cutting needle to sew the chest tube in place. Then I'll repeat the procedure on the other side. Keep an eye on Dr Logan—give him a hand if he needs it.' Dr Logan was working next to her, making cuts through the abdominal wall to determine internal bleeding.

In minutes Marcus had both chest tubes in place. Lisa stood ready with clamps so that when the patient breathed in he did not suck in more air through the tubes, which would again collapse his lungs.

'Got those underwater seals?' Marcus said. 'And the connecting tubing?'

'Yes. . .' Quickly Lisa connected the tubes to other plastic tubes leading to bottles containing water at a certain level so that air could be pushed out of the chest cavity but could not be sucked back in as the patient inhaled.

She watched as water moved up and down the tubes as he inhaled and exhaled. 'So far so good,' she murmured.

'He may need a tracheostomy later,' Marcus added. 'That may be done in the operating room.'

The room seemed like a madhouse as staff came and went, running blood samples to the laboratories, and X-rays were taken of the patient's body. It was organized chaos. Dr Logan was making good progress with the opening into the abdominal cavity.

'The second priority,' Marcus said, 'is to treat shock, that is to stop bleeding. His blood pressure's pretty low. We've got to get that up with intravenous fluids, blood and plasma. We're doing a mini-laparotomy to find out whether he's bleeding into the abdominal cavity, which would most likely be from spleen or liver, or maybe there's a perforated gut. Help Dr Logan with that, Lisa.'

Lisa switched her attention to Dr Logan.

'Put up those skull X-rays, Sadie. . .please,' Marcus called.

'We've informed the operating room that we'll be on our way in a matter of minutes, Dr Blair,' Elsa Graham said.

'Right. He needs to have burr-holes as quickly as possible—there's a cerebral haemorrhage,' Marcus said. 'That's the third priority, Lisa—to treat any problems of the central nervous system. A cerebral haemorrhage can cause a dangerous build-up of pressure on the brain, as I'm sure you know. It can damage the brain irreparably if it isn't relieved quite quickly. First, we have to ensure that he's got adequate circulation. As you know, very low blood pressure from shock can cause acute renal failure and inadequate circulation.'

'Yes.' Lisa nodded. Dr Logan had made a very small abdominal incision.

'I've inserted a plastic tube into the abdominal cavity,' he explained. 'I'm just putting in some sterile intravenous fluid—saline. I then siphon it off. If it comes back blood-stained we know that he has haemorrhage in there. We know whether it's serious, or not so serious, from the amount that comes back. Simple, quick, effective.'

Admiring his skill, Lisa paid close attention. Mentally geared up, she felt ready for anything that they might encounter. Once the patient was stabilized he would be transferred immediately to the operating room where a multidisciplinary surgical team was waiting for him and he would undergo several life-saving operations simultaneously. The neurosurgeons would drill holes in his skull to locate and relieve blood clots which were pressing on the brain, would stop the bleeding.

Someone had inserted a stomach tube into the patient and was aspirating the stomach contents. The orthopaedic resident was splinting the fractured femur which would be operated on later, as well as immobilizing the hip joints because of the fractured pelvis.

Blood, plasma and clear intravenous fluids were running into the patient's veins. He was being given oxygen, hooked up to a ventilator via the endotracheal tube in his throat.

'Get those porters to take him to the OR now, Elsa. There's blood in the abdominal cavity,' Marcus said tersely. 'A lot of it. Get on to the OR again—let them know our findings.'

'The porters are right outside the room, Dr Blair,' Elsa confirmed, going to the double doors of the room to summon them. Two of the residents would accompany their patient to the OR.

'Pass me a couple of the skin clips, please, Lisa, to close this incision,' Ted Logan said. 'I've done all I want to do here.'

'Everyone OK for transfer?' Marcus said, stepping back and looking around him.

There was a general chorus of affirmation.

'Blood pressure's pretty good now,' the anaesthesia resident confirmed, checking his monitors. 'Lungs expanding OK.'

'Right. Let the porters in,' Marcus instructed.

Time moved quickly when life was hectic. The team went immediately from room three to another room to repeat the procedure on a patient who was less seriously injured. There were other teams hurrying about, collecting equipment. Nathan Hanks had his own team. When the emergency was finally over Lisa glanced at a clock, before hurrying back to room three to clear up the mess they had made. She realized as she did so that she would be late home today. She would have to call her mother.

Pushing through the double doors of the resuscitation room, she almost ran smack into Marcus Blair who was coming out. They dodged each other, both stepping sideways in the same direction before bumping into each other. He grabbed her arms.

'Shall we dance?' he said, which was the usual quip in the department when rushing personnel collided, as they frequently did.

Lisa managed a wan smile. When they were not actually interacting at a professional level the atmosphere between them was becoming increasingly equivocal. The doors shut behind her and she could see that there was no one else in the room.

'I've been wanting to tell you,' he said. 'You were great today.'

'Well. . . I. . .I am an OR nurse,' she said quickly. His warm fingers on her arms were all she could think of at that moment. 'Um. . .it's not as though I'm a novice. . . Dr Blair.'

'No. . .' he said, looking down at her. Like hers, his

surgical mask dangled loosely around his neck, revealing the tiredness on his features as his eyes roved over her face.

'When you're with me I always feel somehow responsible for you,' he said, his voice cracking as though his weariness had affected his vocal cords, 'Did you know that?'

'Well. . . No. . .no, I didn't.' The room was very quiet so they could hear the movements of the second hand on the wall clock as it moved jerkily around the clock face. 'I'm really pretty good at looking after myself.'

Marcus let his hands drop to his sides. 'You torment me, Lisa,' he said huskily. 'The memory torments me—of when I first saw you.'

'I. . .I expect it won't last,' she said, searching for words.

'Let's hope it won't,' he said. Abruptly he stepped around her to push through the doors. In a moment he was gone.

Automatically—feeling stunned—Lisa moved to begin the clearing-up and worked at a furious pace—piling dirty instruments into their respective trays, throwing blood-stained linen into plastic bags. She didn't want to think too much, not now. Churned up inside, she didn't want to examine her own emotions. Relief suffused her when Elsa Graham came in to help her.

'Well, Lisa,' Elsa said cheerfully, 'we got through that one OK!'

Preoccupied with thoughts of the patients they had recently dealt with, as well as thoughts about her relationship with Marcus, Lisa was less than alert as she hurried through the front lobby an hour later to return a piece of equipment. It was thus with a jolt of something like horror that she saw a familiar figure passing through the lobby ahead of her.

Among the milling figures that thronged the main lobby she spotted a head of long blonde hair, styled in a ponytail.

Not absolutely sure that it was Charlene Damero, she nonetheless had an awful sinking feeling that it was her. It took Lisa only seconds to decide what she had to do.

'OK!' she said quietly, firmly, out loud to herself. 'I'm absolutely sick of this already. You're not going to terrorize me, if I have anything to do with it!'

She put on her white lab coat which she had handy, tucked her hair up into a surgical cap, put on a clean surgical mask and the glasses that she sometimes wore for reading small print. Briskly she walked round to the waiting room for ambulatory patients. As she walked down the corridor beside it, not pausing in her stride, she glanced in casually.

Yes, there was no mistake. The woman was sitting there sipping coffee from a Styrofoam cup. Her clothing was different from last time, her hairstyle slightly different, yet there could be no mistake. She had the same brilliant red lipstick and carried the same multicoloured bag.

Lisa kept walking, cutting through a connecting door to get back the way she had come. Fear gripped her almost like a physical thing. It seemed ridiculous to be frightened of someone in that way, yet she was. Marcus—and Peter Johanson—had said that this woman could be a psychopath. . .and Lisa felt inclined to agree with them.

A psychopathic person, she reminded herself—as opposed to someone who had a psychosis, a mental illness—could appear perfectly normal a great deal of the time until you really got to know them. They generally had a glibness, a superficiality, a lack of empathy, an ability to manipulate, a charm, when they wanted something from someone. . .often a fatal charm. Lying came as naturally to them as breathing. Criminality was not uncommon with them—neither was murder.

Equally, they could turn nasty in the batting of an eyelid, especially when it became clear to them that they were not going to get what they wanted. In this case, the woman wanted Marcus. Somehow, Lisa doubted that Miss Damero would know what to do with him if she got him—her world was one of fantasy.

Lisa remembered then that there had been several security personnel in evidence when the accident victims had come in. Hurrying back to the lobby, she looked frantically around for one of them. A man she knew only as Doug was still in evidence, even though the crisis was nearly over. In other circumstances, they would have spotted Miss Damero themselves.

'Excuse me. . . Doug?'

'Hi.' He peered at her ID badge. 'Hi, Liz. What can I do for you?'

'Dr Blair spoke to your department on Monday about a woman who had been harassing him by the name of Charlene Damero,' she blurted out breathlessly.

'Yeah, I remember,' he said, looking at her closely. He was a big man, looking very competent in his navy blue uniform. 'She threatened you also, I believe. Yes?'

'That's right,' she confirmed. Doug obviously had made notes of all the details. 'Well, she's in the waiting room over there right now.' Briefly, she gave a description of the woman. 'Maybe we should nip this in the bud before she makes a nuisance of herself. I saw her come in a few moments ago. She manages to avoid the triage nurses.'

'Let me call for some reinforcements,' Doug said, releasing his walkie-talkie from his belt. 'We'll get her from all angles. You make yourself scarce, Liz.'

Marcus wasn't alone when she went to find him in a treatment room. 'Dr Blair,' she said quietly, 'Miss Damero is in the waiting room.'

When he slipped out with her she explained.

'Lisa,' he said wearily, 'come and have a quick cup of coffee with me in my office. It's time we had a break. Everything's under control here.'

'Yes, please,' she agreed, 'I've had nothing since breakfast.'

'OK. I'll tell Sadie where you are so that she won't come looking.'

When he took her elbow, walking swiftly, she didn't resist. Once inside his office he turned to her, after closing the door, his expression serious. 'I must apologize, once again, for all this,' he said, 'I feel pretty awful about it. Hopefully, it won't go on for much longer.'

'I certainly hope not,' she said tiredly. 'It is beginning to get to me, I have to admit that. You said it's been four years she's been harassing you? I don't think I could take four months.'

'This is a battle we'll win, Lisa. It's really my problem. I hate to see you involved. . .in any way.'

'I. . .I am involved, unfortunately, whether I like it or not.'

'Let me get you some coffee.'

The coffee he poured for her was very hot, strong and good.

'Mmm. This is wonderful,' Lisa said, her mind occupied with thoughts of the security personnel escorting the threatening woman from the waiting room. Right now she was glad of the comfort of Dr Blair between her and a sick, nameless fear.

The door burst open and the nurse, Marie, came in. 'Dr Hanks is looking for you, Dr Blair,' she said abruptly, casting a look of surprise at Lisa as she stood leaning against the edge of Marcus's desk. There was veiled hostility in that glance.

'What for, Marie?'

'A consultation in room one.'

'Tell him I'll be there in about three minutes,' Marcus said crisply. 'And, Marie, never enter my office without knocking in future.'

When the nurse had gone Marcus looked at Lisa with an air of apology. 'She tends to get a bit. . .bossy,' he said.

'I've noticed.' Lisa drained her coffee-cup.

'Help yourself to more coffee,' he offered, as he looked at his watch. 'I have to go in a moment. Stay here for a while until we can be sure that Miss Damero has gone.'

'Thank you.' They were both standing, both thinking.

Images of herself as she had appeared to him on the night she had been admitted as an emergency case came to her now that she was alone with him in the small, cramped room. She wished he hadn't made those earlier comments today, which now served to make her self-conscious. He had seen her being undressed, her abdomen palpated, had taken the bag containing her blood-stained clothing, had witnessed her vulnerability. . . That knowledge seemed to hang between them now. It charged the atmosphere with an electric awareness, like the pressure in the air that built up before a storm. Lisa let out a sigh, disturbed by a premonition conjured up by her own analogy.

'Take a taxi home, will you?' Marcus said, 'I'd feel much happier. And do you have a call-display unit on your telephone at home? An answering machine?'

'No to the first question, yes to the second,' she said, suspecting what he might be getting at.

'I recommend that you get one,' he said seriously. 'Don't pick up the receiver unless you recognize the number. Let the machine answer it. Get your father to record the message on your machine. Don't give out your name or address on it. And another thing. . . I've hired a private detective to watch Miss Damero night and day, starting tomorrow, at least until she indicates her next move.'

When he had gone Lisa sat down at his desk to call her mother.

CHAPTER SEVEN

LISA went up to the ward area of Men's Surgical to see Mr Ottinger the next day after her work shift, where she found the patient asleep and a young woman sitting by the bed. Quietly Lisa introduced herself.

'Hi.' The other woman stood up and held out her hand. 'I'm his daughter, Barb Hager.' They both turned to look at the sleeping man. 'He's looking much better than he was at home. They operated on him yesterday—a colostomy. I've been up most of the night with him.'

'His colour is certainly much better than when he came in,' Lisa observed, taking in the details. Mr Ottinger still had a stomach tube in place, and was also getting intravenous fluids. Propped up in the bed, immobile, he still looked very sick.

The daughter motioned Lisa out into the corridor. 'What do you think his chances are?' she asked, fighting back tears. 'I've spoken to the surgeon. He said he has only a few months to live, and that all anyone can really do is make him comfortable as the tumour has spread beyond any sort of control.'

'Well. . .' Lisa began gently, not avoiding eye contact with the other woman, 'I expect he's right, but no one wants to put a time scale on someone else's life. I think you have to assume that, in the long term, he is not going to recover. In the short term it is important to let him know that he's being treated. He needs to have his general health maintained. And, of course, he needs someone to talk to.'

'That's what the young doctor said—Dr Logan,'

Barbara said, wiping away tears. 'That's why he was given the blood transfusion. I'm very glad about that.'

'Yes,' Lisa said firmly, 'and we have a special care ward in this hospital for just such a purpose—so that patients can come in for a few days to be checked and maintained, then go home. It's a very good, hopeful sort of place. Dr Logan will tell you about that.'

'One thing I'm not sure about,' Barbara said hesitantly, 'is whether to tell my mother the news. They're divorced, you see. She knows he has cancer and that he was operated on before. What she doesn't know is that he. . .that he might not have long to live.' She began to sob quietly.

Lisa put an arm round her shoulders, searching for an appropriate answer. What if she were in the daughter's place? What would she do then?

'Would your mother want to come to see him?' she said, finding difficulty in controlling her own emotion. 'And—maybe more important—would he want to see her?'

'Yes,' the daughter said, 'I know my mother still loves him. She. . .she left him because he. . .he drank a lot for years. He was more or less an alcoholic. Then he had an affair with another woman. My mother couldn't take it any more so she left with us kids. That was some years ago, of course.' The tears were flowing freely now as the daughter remembered. 'I've been in two minds about what to do. I think he would want to see her, too.'

'Does he live with the other woman?' Lisa asked gently.

'No,' Barbara Hager said sadly. 'That ended a long time ago. He's alone now. There's me and my brother. . . We're both married and don't live with him, of course.'

'Maybe you should sound out your mother to see if she wants to come,' Lisa said slowly, 'and let her know the seriousness of the situation.'

'Yes. . .I'd better tell her. . . Better break it to her as soon as possible.'

'One of the doctors could talk to her first before she even sees your father. I'm sure Dr Logan would be willing to do that.'

'Yes. Thank you, Nurse.' Barbara made an attempt to smile, 'I feel relieved now.'

'I could speak to Dr Logan,' Lisa offered.

As luck would have it, Ted Logan was at the nursing station at the entrance to the ward as Lisa made her way out. Within minutes she had waylaid him and explained the situation.

'Sure, I'll talk to the guy's ex-wife,' he agreed. 'Sounds to me as though she ought to know. I'll speak to the daughter, too. I'm on my way to see Mr Ottinger as soon as I've written up a few notes here.'

'I'm glad he's being well looked after.'

'One of the staff-men actually queried the blood transfusion we were giving him,' Ted Logan said, running a hand wearily through his short, fair hair. 'He actually said it was a waste of blood and asked me why I was giving it.'

'What did you say?' Lisa asked, sharing his disgust.

'I told him that it makes the patient feel better,' Ted said emphatically. 'I told him that was my number one mandate. I also told him that I didn't know it was hospital policy to write people off. He didn't have anything to say to that. Just walked away.'

'Good for you, Ted,' Lisa said warmly.

'Dr Claibourne's pretty good, but he's so pressured all the time that he's more or less left the day-to-day care of Mr Ottinger to me. If necessary, I'll get Dr Blair to back me up.'

'Yes,' Lisa agreed soberly, 'he'll back you up all the way.'

'You know, I had a patient once who had cancer all over

his body—he was terminal—and the staff-man ordered a blood transfusion to build the guy up a bit. In a few weeks all signs of tumour in that patient had disappeared. No one knew why. It was attributed to the transfusion he had had. Everyone got very excited, of course, and they traced the donor—did all sorts of tests on him.'

'That's amazing. What did they find?'

'Nothing of any significance,' Dr Logan said, 'because they didn't know what they were looking for, of course. They were shooting in the dark.'

It was a beautiful spring day. As Lisa left the hospital to go home her spirits lifted at the sight of the sun shining in a clear blue sky, even though it was not yet very hot. It promised much.

At first she didn't notice the car that crawled next to her along the side of the pavement as she walked briskly away from the hospital, her bag swinging carelessly from one hand. Her thoughts were on Emma Kate—how much she was missing her, how much she longed to pick her up and hug her.

'Hey, bitch!' a voice called, a woman's voice. 'Hey! Hey, you!'

The sound finally got through to Lisa and she stopped. There were a few other people around, though not close enough to hear the words which were directed at her alone.

With a sinking heart Lisa realized she knew the owner of that voice, even before she turned to confirm it.

Charlene Damero was sitting at the wheel of a car, the window wound down on the driver's side. Her long hair hung freely over a skimpy sleeveless top that fitted her tightly, emphasizing her abnormally large breasts. She wore sunglasses.

'You think you're so smart, don't you?' the woman shouted, a sneer in her voice. 'Getting me escorted from the hospital. Let me tell you, that won't work. There's nothing I won't do to be near Marcus. Nothing! Do you hear me?'

Considering carefully for a few seconds, Lisa took two steps towards the car. Bending down so that her face was on a level with the sneering face of the woman, she deftly plucked off the sunglasses, guessing that Charlene would feel more vulnerable without them.

'No, I don't think I'm smart,' she said, slowly, articulating each word carefully—gaining courage from seeing the alarmed eyes which had suddenly been stripped naked, 'but I know I'm smarter than you, Charlene. You're not very bright. If you were you'd know that Marcus Blair feels nothing for you other than a professional concern. You are mentally ill, in need of help.'

'Shut your mouth!' the woman snarled.

'No,' Lisa answered calmly, 'you shut yours. If you keep up this harassment you'll end up in prison again. If you threaten me, in any way, it will just happen sooner. Two came play at this game. You are being watched constantly. Did you know that?'

'What are you talking about?' the woman said derisively.

'A private detective is watching you,' Lisa said, gaining confidence, yet careful not to underestimate this woman in any way. Her kind were unpredictable, dangerous.

'Balls!' Charlene said, then laughed. It was an ugly sound.

'Dr Blair doesn't love you,' Lisa persisted. 'If you were to leave him alone you might find someone who does.'

'Don't give me advice. Don't patronize me. I know what I know.'

'Do you? Next time you do this you'll be arrested.'

'I'll kill anyone who stands in my way.'

Looking briefly sideways—not wishing to take her eyes

off the deranged woman for more than a second—Lisa saw a car approaching them rapidly. It pulled up with a squeal of brakes right behind the car occupied by Charlene Damero, so close that the bumpers nudged.

'What the hell?' Charlene swivelled round and began to hurl verbal abuse at the driver of the other car, who was nonchalantly getting out onto the sidewalk. He was a big man, a very big man.

'That's the private detective I was telling you about,' Lisa said airily, not knowing whether he was or not.

'Liar!' the woman yelled.

A few curious bystanders were beginning to gather. If Lisa hadn't been so frightened she might have laughed hysterically. The absurdity of it seemed out of this world. Yet it was horribly, frighteningly real. Never for one moment should she forget that. It was people who forgot it who ended up dead.

The big man sauntered over, as though he had all the time in the world. He wore a formal, navy blue suit, topped by a trench coat, looking almost a caricature of a private detective. Lisa found herself praying that he was indeed who she hoped.

'Hi,' the man drawled, and bent down to look into the car, giving it the once-over in a very professional manner. Then he very casually put his right hand on his hip, pushing aside his trench coat and jacket to do so. Both women could see very clearly that he had a hand gun in a holster attached to the belt of his trousers.

'Charlene Damero, I believe? I've been watching you.'

Quickly the woman snatched the sunglasses from Lisa's inert hand. 'Leave me alone!' she yelled.

The engine of the car, which had been idling, roared into life as Miss Damero put her foot down on the accelerator. At the same time that the car shot forward the big man put an arm around Lisa and pulled her well clear of the edge of the sidewalk.

They both stood, watching, as the car roared down the street in a cloud of exhaust.

'Are you. . .?' Lisa swallowed. 'Are you who I hope you are?'

'Yeah, I guess I am,' the man confirmed. 'You must be Lisa Stanton. Dr Blair gave me a description of you.' He looked at her very pointedly from head to toe. 'He was sure right in his assessment.' There was an admiring note in his voice.

'You're almost making me laugh,' she said breathlessly, ruefully. 'Yes, I'm Lisa. I'm sure glad to see you!'

'I'll bet,' he agreed, letting his coat fall again to obscure the gun. 'My name's Ravi Davinsky, private investigator. Pleased to meet ya.' He held out a large hand and Lisa gratefully reciprocated.

'Thank you for what you did,' she managed to gasp out, now feeling the full extent of the fear that she had held more or less in check.

'Sorry I wasn't on the scene immediately. I lost sight of her at some traffic lights, but I figured she was heading for the hospital. I didn't want to blow my cover because I wanted to get as much evidence on her as possible,' he explained calmly. 'Evidence of harassment. As soon as we have that we can hand her over to the police. Enough to put her behind bars for a while.'

'I hope you succeed. . .soon.'

'I will,' he said, with an uncommon assurance, gazing up the street where the car had disappeared. Lisa believed him. 'Maybe it's just as well she knows I'm onto her. Let me show you my ID. And I'll tell you something, Lisa. . .' He paused to extract a wallet from his pocket. 'When a man tells you who he is check it out. It's safer, believe me. Especially when he's near a hospital emergency department. For that matter, check out any woman, too. You get all sorts going in there, some of 'em looking for drugs. They seem to think there are going to be drugs just lying about that they can take.'

Looking at his ID badge and photograph, she felt very sober.

'Also, don't mess with a woman like Charlene Damero,' he said. 'She's totally unpredictable. The only predictable thing about her is that she'll be unpredictable, if you'll pardon the lecture. She could dissolve into tears if you confront her, or she could shoot you. Manipulative, that's the word. She'd talk you out of your last dollar bill, if I know anything about psychopaths. . .if that's what we're dealing with here.'

'I see,' Lisa said weakly. Privately, she wasn't sorry she had stood up to the woman.

'Always trust your instincts with people, even if you only get the slightest twinge that something isn't quite right. That twinge could save your life—or at least save you a lot of aggro. Know what I mean?'

'Yes.' Lisa nodded.

'Sure you do! You couldn't be a nurse for very long without having a pretty good idea of what I'm talking about. Just be a bit more careful in this case, that's all.'

Again Lisa nodded. 'How long is this going to take?'

'Not long. I intend to get her,' Ravi Davinsky announced matter-of-factly. 'I've made good progress. If she utters threats, or actually does anything, we'll get her faster than you can say "knife". Then there's the question of her being a public nuisance. Now, Miss Stanton, let me drive you home.'

'What do you think she'll do?' Lisa asked as they got into his car. 'She just said she'd kill anyone who kept her away from Dr Blair.'

'Did she now?'

The private detective looked even bigger as he sat in the car, inspiring confidence. He had thick, black, curly hair that looked as though it was slicked down with oil. His brown eyes were humorous and very, very shrewd, Lisa thought as she observed him considering her question.

'My guess, and it's an educated guess,' he said seriously, 'is that if we hound her enough—and I intend to hound her—she'll suddenly give up. Eventually. These people don't like someone who plays the same game that they're playing themselves. They don't like being the victims. But before she gives up she could get rather ugly. Leave it to me, Miss Stanton.'

Lisa was lying in the bath when the telephone rang. She lay in the scented water with her eyes closed, feeling some of the tension draining away. It had been a trying day. The encounter with Charlene Damero had left her jumpy. At the earliest opportunity she would buy a call-display unit for her telephone.

Wrapping herself in a towel, she padded out to the sitting room and waited to let the answering machine take the call so that she would know who was at the other end.

'Hullo, Lisa,' a welcome voice said.

Quickly she snatched up the receiver, switching off the machine. 'Dr Blair?' she said.

'Yes. I've heard from Ravi Davinsky about the latest encounter. Look, I'm calling to say that I'm going to get you that call-display unit on my way home this evening. I've already ordered one for you. The sooner you get it connected up the better. How are you?'

'I'm all right, thanks,' she confirmed hurriedly, feeling her heart thudding against her ribs and a flush suffusing her skin as though he could actually see her wrapped in a towel. 'I actually stood up to her. . .said a few things that I've been wanting to say. Mr Davinsky told me that

I probably shouldn't have done that, but the satisfaction was great, really great!'

'I'm sure it was,' he said. 'You just take care. Can I see you this evening, Lisa? Would your mother be willing to babysit? I'd like you to come to my house for dinner. We need to talk this over. I'll send a car for you. About seven?'

'I. . . I'd like that very much. Thank you.'

'Have you explained all this to your parents?'

'Yes, I have. All the details, including a description of the woman.'

'Good. See you later, then, Lisa.' Then he was gone, back to the hectic rush of the emergency department, leaving her with a warm feeling of expectation mixed with nervousness at the prospect of being alone with him—really alone with him—for the first time. When he had come to see her Emma had been there between them.

A little later, dressed in jeans and a loose top, she gently picked up her sleeping daughter, who was now quite heavy, and sat cuddling her on the sofa. The first priority in her life was to protect this little human being whom she loved so much. Emma stirred but didn't wake as Lisa nuzzled her cheek, breathing in the scent of soap and baby powder, and softly brushed the fine hair away from her forehead. So far she could see little of Richard in her daughter, nothing of his heavy, masculine features.

As promised, Marcus sent a car for her later.

It turned into a cul-de-sac containing large houses, widely spaced in their own grounds, then finally stopped in the curved driveway of a beautiful, sprawling red-brick house. It was in the downtown part of the city, not far from where she lived herself. Marcus came rapidly down the front steps to meet her. Seeing him, her heart began to pound with an almost fearful expectation, a wild hope.

The evening was still light, with a mellow orange glow from the setting sun.

Then she was being ushered quickly into a spacious hallway and the heavy front door was closed behind them. Surreptitiously she gave a quick look around. Marcus, darkly handsome, wore casual clothing of understated elegance, quality and perfect fit that could only be achieved by a man with a lot of money and impeccable taste to go with it.

'What did you think of Ravi Davinsky?' Marcus asked her, looking at her astutely as he took in her appearance. He seemed very relaxed.

'I was impressed,' she said. As I'm impressed with everything you do, she might have added.

'I think we have reason to be. Let me take your coat.' Marcus smiled at her, his hands on her shoulders, easing the coat off.

At his touch Lisa felt her body stiffen involuntarily. After his remarks to her on the day of the big emergency she found that she was hypersensitive to his nearness.

'You're shivering.' He slipped off her coat. 'Are you cold? We'll get a fire going. We'd turned down the heating since the weather was so great this morning.'

'I. . .I am a little cold,' she lied. In truth, she was shaking with nerves.

Seeing Marcus now in the setting of his very sophisticated home, her suspicion was confirmed that he was out of her league and that she should not assume that his interest in her was more than a gentlemanly one. This sober admission was depressing. He was primarily concerned for her safety, she reminded herself. . .even though he was, she sensed, drawn to her sexually. It was there in the veiled light of his glance and in the brooding way he watched her.

There was a reluctance in him. Lisa could sense that,

too. He wasn't a man who would indulge his desires thoughtlessly. Not like Richard, who would seduce a woman on a whim. More than ever, she reminded herself, she must not been seen to presume, otherwise she could be mortified if he rejected her. Was she presuming? Sometimes she was so confused that she wasn't sure.

Not for the first time, she reminded herself that a man in his position, who would have a wide choice of women, would hardly be drawn to a woman who had another man's child. An odd longing took possession of her.

As he turned away to hang up her coat in a capacious closet by the front door Lisa almost expected a butler to appear in the panelled hall and offer her a drink on a silver tray. 'Come into the sitting room for a drink, Lisa,' Marcus offered, taking her arm to walk with her down the wide hall to a door on their left. 'Our dinner is more or less ready so we've just got time for a glass of sherry, or whatever you'd like. A cocktail, perhaps?'

'Sherry would be perfect,' she said, hoping she was hiding the fact that she was beginning to feel somewhat overwhelmed by the house—and by the man.

When they entered a beautiful sitting room with huge paintings on the walls and exquisite furniture and lamps, made welcoming by vases of fresh flowers and potted plants, Lisa was very glad that she had taken trouble with her appearance and had rejected her original plan of wearing jeans and a sweater.

She wore a soft chemise dress in a fine chocolate-coloured wool which had long sleeves and a cowl neck, with opaque tights and suede shoes to match the dress. Equally, she had been careful with her make-up, knowing that her subtle grey eyeshadow enhanced her large blue eyes and that a bronze lipstick added welcome colour to her pale face.

'Did you cook the dinner?' she ventured, as he poured the drinks.

'No.' He turned to give her an assessing look as she stood in the middle of the vast room, where her shoes sank into the pile of the oriental rug. 'I inherited a cook from my parents.'

His glance was undeniably masculine as he took in her appearance, his eyes roving unselfconsciously over her. Lisa felt the heat rising in her face as he handed her a glass of sherry and stood near her.

'I'm mindful that tomorrow is a working day for both of us,' he said, very much in command of the situation, 'so unfortunately we can't linger for very long, I know. But I wanted to see you—outside of work.' The way he said it set up a small hope in her that this was not just a duty invitation because he felt responsible for her. With telling insight she knew that she wanted and needed that.

'I'm glad you did,' she said quietly.

'I have the call-display unit for you,' he said. 'When I take you home later I'll set it up for you.'

'Thank you,' she said.

'I'm very sorry it's necessary,' he said.

Lisa shrugged. There was a silence between them, which she sought desperately to fill, yet could think of nothing to say. Normally their silences were reasonably comfortable ones. There was so much to say, yet little that she could actually put into words at this moment.

'You. . .you're very lucky to have a cook,' she said at last.

'Don't I know it.' He laughed, moving a little away from her so that she let out the breath she realized she had been holding. 'I took over this house from my parents, with most of the contents, when they recently decided they wanted a much smaller place and would like to spend every winter in the Caribbean. This is where I grew up, apart from a few forays abroad. The cook wanted to stay on so I let her.'

'Do you have a butler?' she asked facetiously, gaining confidence.

'No.' He grinned, the action lighting up his ruggedly attractive face. 'I hire one from an agency when I need one.'

'Oh, do you?' She smiled. 'You're beginning to intimidate me. You're not the Dr Blair I know at work.'

'And you're not the Lisa Stanton I know from the hospital,' he countered. 'You look very lovely. Perhaps I should say. . .more lovely.'

She shrugged again. 'Thank you.'

'Come and sit down, Lisa.' With a motion of his arm he indicated a voluminous sofa near the baronial fireplace.

Hastily she sipped her sherry when she was seated, deciding that she needed the courage that it afforded. If she wasn't careful she'd make a fool of herself with Marcus Blair. Already she felt herself shivering with a delightful—and fearful—anticipation whenever he came within two yards of her. As she drank he knelt down and put a match to the newspapers and kindling which were in the fireplace.

To her relief, he took a seat opposite her when the flames were leaping warmly around the wood.

'Tell me more about yourself, Lisa,' he invited softly. 'I'm curious.'

'I can't imagine why,' she said, forcing a lightness to her tone. 'Are you vetting me or something? Trying to find out if I'm worthy of the efforts of your cook?'

'Maybe.' He smiled slowly, his eyes on her face. 'Go on.'

'There isn't much to tell. As you know, I grew up in the house I live in now. My childhood was ordinarily happy, with super parents. I have an older sister who works in Ottawa and an older brother who lives in Vancouver—he works in the film industry.'

'So you're the baby of the family,' he murmured.

'Yes...' she said, lowering her eyes before his astute gaze. The word 'baby' brought thoughts of her own baby, never far from her mind, sharply into focus. From the silence that ensued she sensed that he was thinking of her too.

When the silence lengthened so that she could no longer bear it, while he looked at her openly, she blurted out, 'Why did you invite me here, Marcus? You can't exactly be short of female company. We could have said all we have to say on the telephone about the dreadful situation that you're in...and that I seem to be in now, too.'

'I wanted to see you in person to talk about the problem,' he said, unabashed. 'Is that good enough?' There was innuendo in his tone, as though there was more than one problem.

'I'm not sure,' she said, blundering on, the sexual tension unmistakable between them. 'Why do you look at me...as though you want to...?'

'What?'

'I don't know. I...know this may sound crude...' She bit her lip convulsively before continuing, 'I hope you don't think that because I've had a baby without being married that I'm...that I'm what you might call a...' She couldn't go on.

'An easy lay?' he offered.

Her face flushed. 'Something like that,' she said painfully.

'You mean exactly that,' he said.

With lithe ease he got up to put a few logs on the blazing fire, then he came over to her and she found herself holding her breath again. Kneeling down in front of her, he took both her hands in his.

'You *are* cold,' he said, squeezing her hands briefly and then letting them go. 'Lisa, I don't think of you that way. Having a baby outside marriage doesn't have the same connotations that it used to have in our parents' generation, particularly in a city.' He got up and walked to the fireplace restlessly, half turned away from her. 'I look at you because you're a remarkably attractive woman. I can't help myself.'

There was a loaded silence in the room, filled fitfully by the crackling of the fire.

'I'm sorry. I know I'm defensive. I can't help it yet,' she said. Having told herself not to presume with him, she seemed to have done just that.

Abruptly, he came and sat near her on the sofa. She looked down at her clasped hands as the subtle scent of his cologne filled her nostrils, his proximity disturbing.

'Has Richard Decker destroyed all your confidence as a woman?' he asked softly, very close to the mark. When she didn't answer he went on, 'I invited you here because I want your company,' he said levelly. 'I'm a lonely man. My social life at the moment is about nil. Too much work, not enough time to make social contacts. So, you see, I have no ulterior motive.'

A knock came on the door, and after a few moments an elderly woman with a shock of pure white hair peered around it as Marcus stood up and called, 'Come in!'

'Your dinner's ready, Mr Marcus. Shall I serve it now?'

'Thanks, Anne. Just give us five minutes, would you?' Marcus said.

'Okey-doke, Mr Marcus.'

Marcus smiled at her crookedly. 'Enough talking for now. Finish that sherry, Lisa,' he said. 'I think you need it.'

As Lisa drank the sherry she had a depressing feeling that she might have made a fool of herself. In her efforts to be open and honest she had—rather clumsily, she felt now—made the assumption that he would find her acceptable as a lover.

The dinner was superb, as was the wine Marcus served with it. Bit by bit Lisa found her defences melting as one course followed another. After a hesitant start, the wine worked its magic and conversation was no problem. They talked about themselves, and everything else under the sun—except Charlene Damero. That, by tacit agreement, would come later. Likewise, the silences became easier.

The dining room, with its huge table and sideboards, was almost as big as the sitting room they had vacated. A glittering chandelier hung low over the table.

'Come on,' Marcus said, rising to his feet to serve their final course. 'We'll eat our dessert and have coffee in the sitting room by the fire.'

Lisa glanced at her watch. 'Oh, my God! It's almost half past nine. I didn't realize. I have to feed Emma at ten. I. . .I really must go very soon. This is a fantastic dinner. Thank you so much. But I'll have to forgo the coffee, if you don't mind.'

'Give me coffee at your place,' he said smoothly. 'That will save us time since I'm going to drive you back.'

In no time at all they were in Marcus's car and driving swiftly back to the part of the city where she lived, a distance of about two miles, leaving behind them a delectable jumble of used dishes and wine glasses in the impressive dining room.

'Would you like me to make the coffee?' Marcus offered, once they were back at her flat.

Lisa, who couldn't help making the comparison between her small flat and his spacious house, hesitantly agreed. The wine had relaxed her.

Mrs Stanton had made herself scarce as soon as they

arrived, and Emma Kate was just beginning to work up a righteous anger. Quickly Lisa changed her clothes and began to feed her baby.

After about fifteen minutes a slight noise brought Lisa's attention to the half-open doorway of Emma's tiny room.

'Would you like your coffee in here?' Marcus asked, from where he was leaning against the doorframe.

'How long have you been there?' she asked, as a wave of familiar heat ran swiftly through her. From where she sat, partially turned away from the door, he could get a good view of her, breast-feeding Emma Kate.

'Long enough. . .' There was a note of wry amusement in his voice. Awareness seemed to crackle between them as he continued to lean there, and she went on feeding Emma, outwardly calm.

'I'll have my coffee later, thanks, in the kitchen,' she said, her voice tight. 'I won't be much longer.'

His eyes seemed to bore into her as she quickly returned his glance, yet he didn't move from the doorway—didn't invade her privacy any further. There was a barely contained energy in him, and strange vibes that she could not interpret. Silently he withdrew, and she breathed more easily.

Then the thought came to her of how Richard had taken her that last time—thoughtlessly, as though he had a right. That had been the way he did everything—going for what he wanted and just taking it.

When Emma was in bed they talked in the sitting room over coffee about their security and about what Ravi Davinsky wanted to do, before handing over to the police. As they talked, Marcus attached the new call-display unit to her telephone.

'Essentially,' Marcus said, making a move to leave, 'he wants to get enough evidence—with witnesses, if possible—to build a good case against her. She's breaking the restraining order, for one thing. Everything's in hand.'

'I feel safer with that gadget,' Lisa said as she went to open a window to let in a little fresh air. 'Thank you for getting it.'

'That's the least I can do.' He was on his feet, ready to go. 'I feel responsible for getting you into this, Lisa... however inadvertently.'

'My number's not actually in the book, but she could probably get it without too much trouble.' The sitting room window faced the street. Darkness had fallen and in the dim light of the streetlamps Lisa could see Marcus's car parked in front of the house. Now that he was ready to go she felt ambivalent about his going, feeling a surge of anticipated loneliness, even though her parents were just through the connecting door.

'Don't answer any numbers that aren't familiar to you. Let the machine answer,' he said with authority. 'If we're lucky we could get her on tape, although she's so damned devious I doubt that she'd actually leave a message.'

As she stood looking through the window, down to the street, Marcus came up behind her. 'Try not to worry too much,' he said. 'We've done all we can for now. Goodnight, Lisa.'

'Goodnight, Marcus. And...and thank you. For the wonderful dinner.'

'My only regret is that you've been drawn into this utter madness—.' He stopped, looking down at her.

'It's not as bad as being in the surgical pits in Somalia,' she said, in an attempt at lightness. 'In those awful hot tents, wondering if you'll ever leave the country alive... waiting for dawn...trying to identify at least some of the sounds outside...'

'Mmm... Puts everything into perspective, doesn't it...?' His voice was barely audible as he looked at her with a taut expression, a slight frown between his dark brows.

'Well, goodnight, then,' she said again. 'I. . .I'll see you to the door.'

Instead, she didn't move because he seemed to will her not to—seemed to compel her to stay within his orbit.

'Yes. . . Goodnight,' he murmured. Slowly he put his hands up to her face, one on each side, cupping her cheeks with his warm fingers. The room was silent, the house quite still. He stroked a thumb delicately over her lips and she trembled with an exquisite anticipation. Immobilized, she waited, her breathing shallow.

As his head came down slowly towards hers she closed her eyes, unable to sustain the intensity of their silent visual exchange. When his mouth touched hers a sensation of such exquisite pleasure swept through her that she gave a muffled cry of longing. She couldn't move, couldn't obey the vague dictate of her conscious mind that she ought to move away from him. She stood inert, her body tingling with shock at his touch.

He didn't bring his body in contact with hers: only his hands on her face held her captive while his mouth took possession of hers, his firm lips moving sensuously over hers so that she felt totally lost in him. So often she had wondered what it would be like to be kissed by him. The reality was so much more devastating than the fantasy had been. Time seemed to stand still in a moment of utter perfection. . . She wanted this contact never to end. . .

Again and again he raised his mouth from hers, brushing her lips tantalizingly with his—teasing her, yet never quite breaking contact. She found herself daring to respond and tentatively kissed him back, responding to that hopeful fluttering of renewed trust within her, even as she sensed intuitively that he was kissing her because he couldn't help himself, that it wasn't something he had planned.

The knowledge that he desired her filled Lisa with a wild exhilaration. At the same time a warning voice spoke in her head those awful words, 'an easy lay', and told her that sexual desire didn't, of itself, always mean a great deal. Richard had taught her that. An 'easy lay'. . . She had never been that.

Then she felt him stiffen as he pulled back from her, and he lowered his hands to her shoulders. 'Hell!' he muttered.

Lisa's eyes snapped open, to find Marcus looking over her head out of the window. He was frowning.

'What?' she asked. 'What is it?'

'There's a car down there, right behind mine. Too close to mine to be parking. There are no other parked cars on the street. The lights are on and there's someone in it,' he said tensely. 'It could be our friend, Miss Damero.'

Lisa turned quickly, feeling Marcus's restraining hands on her shoulders. 'Oh, no!' she said, her feeling of warm relaxation giving way to apprehension.

'Careful,' he said, gripping her. 'Stay back. If it is her I don't want her to see more than she has already.'

'That car wasn't there a few moments ago when I opened the window,' Lisa said. 'Do you think she's been watching us? If it is her.'

'Probably,' he said, a note of disgust in his voice. 'Come away. I'm going to phone Ravi—see if if he's lost sight of her.' As he strode over to the telephone Lisa sat on the edge of the sofa and did a mental inventory of her doors and windows, assuring herself that they were securely locked or latched.

While Marcus talked she restlessly went back over to the window to stand partially behind a curtain and watch the street, trying to get the registration number of the car.

'Marcus,' she called in a soft voice, 'it's leaving.'

'See if you can get the number.'

'No. . .no, I couldn't.' She turned to him as he came to her. 'Thank God it's gone. What did Mr Davinsky say?'

'She's been using hired cars. Never the same one twice, apparently. She doesn't own a car,' Marcus said tensely. 'They've been watching her apartment. She doesn't park the hired cars there so it's possible that she could have slipped out. . .maybe the back way. But they don't think so because they've been watching that, too.'

Lisa sighed. 'What are we going to do?'

'I'll spend the night here on the sofa. If you don't mind, that is. I would feel happier. Just in case it was her.' He passed a hand tiredly over his face, pressing the tips of his fingers against his eyelids for a moment. 'I doubt that it was her, but we won't take any chances. I'll feel happier if I'm here.'

'All right. So will I,' she agreed, knowing that he was trying to reassure her, probably convinced that it was Miss Damero. 'I'll get you a pillow and a duvet.'

'We'd both better get some sleep,' he said. 'I'll see myself out in the morning.'

Later in the night Lisa woke, stirring restlessly in the bed as she remembered that Marcus was there a few yards away from her. The fluorescent hands of the bedside clock pointed to 2 a.m. There was no sound from Emma Kate, who sometimes still woke in the middle of the night.

Lisa got up, and padded on bare feet downstairs to the sitting room. Marcus lay on his back, the duvet pulled down to reveal his naked chest. In the dim light from the street she could see the dark hair that covered the centre part of it. His head, with its dark, unruly hair, was turned away from her. Slowly her eyes travelled over his firm jaw and sensuous mouth, down over the full length of his body. At that moment she longed to pull aside the cover and crawl in beside him, feel his arms coming round her. . .

Frustrated, she turned away from him to check on Emma. Marcus had to be up early, as did she.

CHAPTER EIGHT

THE emergency department was as busy as it could be during the next week, with a rash of minor accidents. The weather had turned decisively warmer, from quite cold to quite hot, over a few days. There was little time during working hours for Lisa to dwell on her private life and problems.

'How you doing, Lisa?' Diane Crane queried as they passed each other at great speed in the corridor. The orientation period for both of them was now over—they were part of the team.

'Trying to keep a low profile.' Lisa smiled at her friend as she followed a stretcher case that had just come in by ambulance. 'No good, though.'

With a wave of her hand she indicated to the ambulance attendants that they should turn into an examination cubicle. They in turn gave her some quick background information. The patient on the stretcher was a girl of about seventeen, accompanied by her distraught parents.

As Lisa stood back, waiting for the ambulance attendants to make the transfer, Diane came back to speak to her. 'Listen,' she whispered, grasping Lisa's arm, 'I've heard something about that gorgeous Dr Blair, a bit of gossip. Try to get your coffee-break with mine. I'll tell you all the details. Apparently, he was engaged to be married—to Dr Lydia Grenville, no less. I've worked with her. She ought to have been in films, not in medicine. . . absolutely stunning.'

'There won't be anything left to tell,' Lisa grinned, trying to keep her face neutral as her heart gave an uncomfortable little jump at the mention of Marcus. Her interest was captured, in spite of her basic aversion to gossip.

'There's more,' Diane muttered. 'She wouldn't wait for him when he had to go to Africa for three months, so the story goes. What a dingbat, eh? I'd sure wait for him.' Her eyes were dreamy. 'Or that cute Nathan Hanks.'

'I've got to go, Diane. This is my patient.'

'OK, Liz. See you in the coffee room later. Bye.'

'Tell me what happened, and when,' Lisa said to the girl's parents in the examination cubicle, a folder of papers ready in her hand with forms for laboratory tests that might have to be done. This appeared to be a change from the usual accidents. 'This is your daughter, Susan, seventeen years old? And you are Mr and Mrs Bowlder?'

'Yes.' The father nodded. He was a tired-looking, middle-aged man, thin and stooped and going bald. Lisa felt a wave of compassion for him and his wife, getting the impression that this was their only child. 'Last night she started throwing up, real bad.'

'Couldn't keep anything down,' his wife, who was equally thin, chipped in. She looked exhausted.

'Then she started behaving strange,' the father continued. 'Like getting mad with us when we asked her what was wrong, and how she felt. She wouldn't let us touch her, like take her temperature, or anything.'

'She's very irritable, just wanting to sleep all the time. I think there's something really wrong with her. She's been thrashing out at us when all we want to do is find out how she's feeling.' Mrs Bowlder took up the story, tears in her eyes.

'She sort of looks at us as though she doesn't know who we are,' Mr Bowlder said. 'She has this sort of glassy-eyed look. . . See for yourself. She just mumbles when we speak to her.'

The girl, Susan, was staring up at the ceiling, her eyes wide, as though she wasn't really focusing on anything. From where Lisa stood, next to the bed, she could see that the girl's pupils were dilated. She took her penlight torch from her pocket and shone the beam of light into the girl's eyes, noting that the pupils contracted very slightly but still remained abnormally expanded. There was definitely a cerebral problem.

'I'm going to take her temperature,' Lisa said, 'then I'll get our doctor to see her.'

As Lisa felt for Susan's pulse she noted that the girl's hands were cold and clammy. Carefully, quickly, she charted her findings. Later she would enter all this into a computer.

'Susan?' Lisa said, bending over the girl. Susan said nothing, just continuing to stare at the ceiling. Then, as they watched, her body twitched slightly.

'Has that happened before?' Lisa asked urgently.

'Yes, this morning,' the mother said. 'That's why we called the ambulance. Didn't bother to call the doctor. We figured we ought to come straight here.'

'You did the right thing. Tell me,' Lisa said urgently, 'has she been sick in the last week or so? Flu? A viral infection of some sort?'

'Well. . .yes,' the mother confirmed, half-fearfully. 'Last week she stayed home from school for four days. . . didn't feel well. Sort of like flu, but not as bad. We did call the doctor. He said to come in to the office but she didn't go because she was so tired. We all figured it would get better on its own. And she did seem better for a couple of days. . . Started eating again.'

'Then the vomiting started?' Lisa queried as she stood beside the bed in her neat white pants suit, her pen poised to make notes of anything that might be important and to take the main points of the history.

'Yes.'

'Her temperature's a little below normal,' Lisa confirmed, after checking. A suspicion had formed in her mind, and was growing stronger, that the girl might have Reye's syndrome, an often deadly syndrome that could come on after a viral infection. The glassy, staring eyes were one indicator. The irritability her parents had described could be a manifestation of swelling of the brain tissue.

'I'll call the doctor now. We'll soon get this sorted out,' she said reassuringly to the parents. 'Have a seat just here.'

Picking up the internal telephone, she put a call through to the triage station. 'Dr Blair to cubicle eight, please,' she said to the nurse who answered.

While she waited for Marcus to come she got together the equipment that she knew would be needed—the intravenous lines and bags of fluid, syringes and tubes for the blood samples that they would have to take to send to the laboratory. With the glass tubes, she lined up the appropriate request forms for the lab.

'Hi.' Marcus arrived, coming into the small room like a whirlwind, his white coat flapping over his green scrubsuit. 'What can I do for you here?'

'Mr and Mrs Bowlder.' Lisa introduced the parents in her best professional voice, determined that her private interaction with Marcus would not affect her working skills in any way. 'And this is Susan, their daughter.'

Marcus smiled, inclining his head to the parents. Quickly Lisa gave him a summary of the symptoms then, while he questioned Mr and Mrs Bowlder further, she made sure that everything was on hand for an examination. The girl herself seemed unable to answer or fully understand the questions that they put to her, an alarming sign.

'Shall I call the intern, Dr Blair?' Lisa asked.

'Yes. I want three IV lines put up. Start on that yourself,

would you? Get the intern to help with that,' Marcus said, sizing up the situation quickly as he began a systematic physical examination of the patient. 'But before you do that, Liz, get on to the blood bank and order three units of fresh frozen plasma, stat.'

'Could this be Reye's?' she said quietly.

'Very likely,' he said tersely, 'so I want those IV fluids up right away—one litre of dextrose to start. These patients are hypoglycaemic and there's liver damage so the sooner we get some sugar into them, the better.'

'Right,' Lisa said, going to the telephone to call the blood bank. Then she put on a pair of rubber gloves to insert the first cannula into a vein for the IV fluid, while Marcus continued with the examination as he talked. Susan responded only sluggishly to neurological stimuli.

'I also want IV mannitol put up,' Marcus instructed her, 'to reduce the cerebral swelling. We'll put saline through the third IV line until we get the plasma from the lab. Also, please have the neurology resident paged right away—we'll get him to order an emergency CAT scan, just to rule out anything else.'

'OK.'

At the telephone again, she called the locating service.

'Neurology resident to Emergency right away, please. Cubicle eight. Patient Susan Bowlder. Thanks.'

Quickly she and Marcus worked side by side, involving the anxious parents in their explanations. The mother was openly crying now, while the father looked desperately pale and worn.

When the intern, Abby Gibson, arrived she silently stripped off her white coat and waited for instructions.

'Abby, take some blood, would you?' Marcus said, looking up from his task with a stethoscope dangling from his ears. 'I want tests for blood-sugar, prothrombin time, liver function, serum aminotransferases. This could be a

Reye's syndrome—they get liver and renal damage, as well as cerebral oedema.'

'Generally following a viral infection, right? Exacerbated by the taking of aspirin?' Abby Gibson said, putting a needle on a syringe preparatory to taking blood.

'That's right,' Marcus said. 'Then, when you've done that, help Liz with the IVs. The patient's dehydrated so we want to get that fluid into her as quickly as possible. No doubt her blood-sugar's way down.'

What Marcus did *not* say, in front of the parents, was that there was no specific cure for Reye's syndrome. All they could do was treat the symptoms and hope that the treatment had been started in time before the brain damage, as well as the liver and kidney damage, had gone too far to be reversed.

The three of them worked on her while the fearful parents watched in silence. Within minutes there were three IV lines functioning—two in the backs of Susan's hands and one in a vein at her ankle.

Marcus straightened. 'Definitely looks like Reye's syndrome to me. There's definitely neurological involvement,' he said quietly to Abby and Lisa. 'I'm going to arrange to have her admitted right away to the critical care unit. They may prefer to have an IV line in her neck—we'll let the neurology resident do that up there.'

The two women exchanged glances, both knowing that this cluster of symptoms they were witnessing—which generally followed a viral infection for no known reason—had a fifty per cent chance of being fatal. Perhaps they had got Susan just in time; perhaps the IV mannitol they were giving her would sufficiently reduce the cerebral swelling before permanent brain damage ensued.

'This syndrome is generally seen in kids of fifteen and under, isn't it?' Abby Gibson asked Marcus.

'Yes, but it can affect older teenagers, as you see. Cases

have been described. I'll get one of the medical staff-men to see her as well when she gets up to the unit. Maybe they'll do the CAT scan on the way up,' Marcus went on. 'We'll keep her here until we get the fresh plasma delivered. If it's not here in the next five minutes, Liz, maybe you could get on to the lab again. They are going to deliver it here, I take it?'

'Yes, that's the usual procedure,' Lisa confirmed.

While Marcus made a few telephone calls Lisa and the intern carefully labelled the blood samples and filled in the request forms, marking each one 'stat'. 'The guy who brings the plasma can take these tubes back to the lab with him,' Abby said.

Marcus sat down with the parents and unhurriedly began to explain the situation to them and discuss the planned treatment. Again, Lisa marvelled at his skill in dealing with people. He seemed to understand instinctively just what they were feeling and the kind of questions they would want answered, never rushing them.

The three units of plasma arrived, brought by a lab runner, just as Lisa was about to call them again. While Abby replaced a bag of IV saline with one of plasma for their patient Lisa handed over the blood samples.

'She'll be going to Critical Care,' she explained to the lab runner. 'Could you put the results on the computer to us, and to them, please?'

'Sure.'

Busying herself with clearing up the debris, Lisa considered that they had done all they could do for the moment.

Susan was a pretty girl, about average in height and weight, with long, soft, fair hair and large blue eyes. Now that the immediate crisis was over they could talk to her parents to fill in details of the family background and medical history. The intern would do a great deal of that.

With medical skill—and luck—the girl might survive.

Marcus came to stand next to her to check the running of the IV fluids. 'They may want to give her steroids when she gets up to Critical Care,' he commented quietly. 'There's a fair amount of liver damage with this. They'll put in a urinary catheter when she gets there too. They'll want to know her fluid intake and output, with the possibility of kidney damage.'

'What causes some kids to get this, and some not, when they've had exactly the same illness?' Lisa queried, looking down with sadness at the girl's pale face—at the eyes that were now closed.

'It's not clear.' Marcus sighed. 'Hypoglycaemia may have something to do with it. Anyone with a child sick with a viral infection should make sure they have plenty of fluids—and sugar if they aren't eating—before they get to the vomiting stage, which is indicative of Reye's.'

Porters arrived soon after to take Susan to the critical care unit. The intern would accompany her and her parents.

'With luck, she'll be OK,' Marcus commented as the others disappeared towards the department elevators, leaving him and Lisa watching them.

'I sure hope so,' she said.

Lisa began to clear up the room. She hadn't been alone with Marcus since he had been at her flat early the other morning, at which time they had both been so rushed to get to work on time that they had said very little to each other. All interaction since had been strictly professional, and the nuances had been such that Lisa felt he was keeping a distance from her. Perhaps he regretted their moments of intimacy, regretted that he had initiated those devastating kisses. For her part, she felt obsessed by the memory.

'Are there any new developments, Dr Blair?' she said tentatively, not sure that this was the right time, yet having no idea when she would have another opportunity to speak to him alone. 'From Ravi Davinsky?'

'I've spoken to him a couple of times,' he confirmed. 'He and his men are watching her like hawks. He doesn't think that could have been her the other night, watching your place, but he can't be completely sure. He does have other jobs on hand that he has to take care of.'

'I sure hope it wasn't,' she said feelingly.

'Hey,' he said, 'don't look so agonized. We've got a lot of people looking out for her, if you count the security people here as well.'

'I know,' she said ruefully, 'but you know what a zoo this place is frequently. Sometimes I think half the mafia could get in here with machine-guns and start a shoot-out before anyone realized.'

He laughed, showing his perfect teeth, a light in his eyes. Just then the internal telephone rang. 'Dr Blair here,' he answered it. 'Sure. I'll be right there.' With a quick salute of his hand, he was gone.

As she quickly finished the clearing-up Lisa realized, with a kind of fearfulness, that she was getting more and more emotionally involved with Marcus Blair, and that her feelings were all mixed up with those she still retained for Richard Decker.

Going quickly to the nurses' coffee-lounge for a few minutes' break, she found Diane there. 'Hi.' She smiled. 'I'm desperate for a bit of caffeine.'

While she poured herself coffee into a Styrofoam cup she filled Diane in on what she had been doing.

Then Diane butted in. 'You know that Dr Lydia Grenville I mentioned before—engaged to Marcus Blair?' Diane said, eager to return to the subject. 'Well, they were both working at Gresham General about three years ago and he was crazy about her, so the gossip goes. One of the other nurses here used to work there with them.'

Gresham General was another teaching hospital in the city. Lisa sipped her coffee, wrapped in her own thoughts and feelings. Those feelings told her that she was reluctant to consider Marcus Blair's past, as though he had only existed from the moment she had seen him in the hospital parking lot when she had needed help. In that way, she could somehow think of him as belonging to her. . .and to her baby. He didn't, of course. It was a comforting fantasy sometimes when she felt alone.

'They say she got fed up because he kept going off to remote places with International Physicians. She didn't want to go with him,' Diane went on eagerly. 'Then, when he was away one time, she upped and married someone else—some big shot, one of the chief executive officers at the hospital. She hadn't even told Dr Blair. He came back to find her married.'

'Sad,' Lisa murmured, 'very sad. . .'

When she got back to the triage station Sadie Drummond came up to her.

'I want you to deal with one of our AIDS patients, John Clarkson, when he comes in at lunchtime,' she said. 'We have an AIDS group support clinic here in the ambulatory section once every two weeks. It's run by one of the medical guys who spends at lot of his time dealing with AIDS patients these days. He makes himself available to them every day. Anyway, John Clarkson often comes up here to talk to Dr Blair as well, in between times, when he gets depressed. He usually makes an appointment, just to make sure that Dr Blair can see him.'

'I see,' Lisa said. 'I'd like to meet him.'

'Take him along to Dr Blair's office when he comes. He usually sees him there. Get his chart from our files and read something about him.'

* * *

John Clarkson was a thin, wiry young man, looking younger than his thirty years in spite of the tiredness on his features. Lisa made sure that she was there when he checked in at the triage station.

In the interim, she had managed to read something of his tragic story. A haemophiliac, he had contacted the AIDS virus from a blood transfusion some years before. Although he already had the active disease he seemed to be holding his own so far, and was undergoing treatment at University Hospital with experimental drugs, as well as with nutritional and vitamin therapy.

'I'm Liz.' She introduced herself with her departmental official name, without supposing that John Clarkson would ever pose any sort of danger to her. 'I'm going to be your nurse from now on. I understand that your regular nurse is off on maternity leave?'

'Yeah. . . Hi,' he said. 'Is Dr Blair going to see me?' There was a restless, anxious quality about him, his movements quick and nervous and his eyes dull. His hands were stained with brown patches of nicotine.

Lisa's heart went out to him as she smiled warmly. 'Oh, yes,' she said. 'He's expecting you right now.' She tried not to let the sympathy show on her face. Once someone had told her that sympathy was what you gave to people when you had nothing more to give them.

'We'll go to his office now,' she said. 'Do you mind if I'm present when he sees you?'

'Nope,' he said, 'I guess not. So long as you don't make me feel like some sort of exhibit—or some sort of teaching tool. I don't like being patronized either, like the walking dead or something.'

'I wouldn't do any of those things,' she assured him as they walked down the corridor to Marcus's office. 'Although I have to confess that I don't really know a lot about AIDS because I worked in the operating rooms before I started in the emergency department so we never knowingly met a patient with it.'

'But you had to treat everyone as though they had it, right?'

'Yes,' she confirmed. 'You probably know much more about it than I do.'

'You're probably right. I've read a lot of books, talked to a lot of people. When your life's on the line you do that.'

For the next three quarters of an hour she sat quietly in the background in Marcus's office while he and John talked. John unburdened himself—talked about his difficulties and his fears, going over the details of his treatment, anything that he did not fully understand.

Several times Lisa bit her lip hard, clenched her hands tight, to prevent tears filling her eyes. Through no fault of his own this young man had a deadly disease to contend with on top of his underlying blood-clotting problem. From what he was telling Marcus, his parents were suffering from trying to come to terms with all this, and he was trying to help them while helping himself.

She marvelled at how Marcus listened, how he answered John, giving him his full attention and never butting in or hurrying him up as some doctors did. She had even seen doctors who looked at their watches openly in front of patients, or who tapped a foot impatiently when someone needed desperately to talk.

Listening didn't make money, she thought cynically, in this day and age of ever-tightening budgets. Then there was the question of individual greed, a sin to which doctors were not immune when they charged the health system on a per capita patient basis a fee for service.

'Did you learn anything from that?' Marcus asked her when they had said goodbye to their patient.

'Oh, yes,' she confirmed, 'lots.'

Not least, she was learning more and more about Marcus

Blair. Her initial opinion of him was being confirmed. Respect and admiration were uppermost in her mind—as well as more personal feelings which she dared not dwell on now and that she deliberately pushed further from her mind.

'This is another case of not writing someone off,' he said. 'With all the intensive research that's going on around the world something could come up any day now that could cure this disease.'

Later, when she was going off duty, passing through the front office area, she saw Marcus with the intern, Abby Gibson. They were standing close together, shoulders touching, and they were looking at the computer print-out of the lab results on Susan Bowlder. The CAT scan results would probably be available, too. Lisa felt a sharp stab of jealousy at the sight of them together, an unfamiliar feeling that shocked and annoyed her. She doubted that Marcus lead a celibate life. Hastily, she averted her eyes from them.

She knew that getting involved with a doctor could mean a lifetime of waiting around for some attention from him. Goodness knows, Richard had had very little time for her, really. He had taken from her, had made sure she was there for him. It would be madness to accept that sort of life again, even if it were on offer. . .

Forcing herself to concentrate on other things, she hurried to the critical care unit and located Susan Bowlder. Instantly she could see from the faces of the parents, as they sat beside the bed, that the situation had improved. Their expressions lightened even more as they recognized her.

'How is she?' Lisa whispered. The girl appeared to be sleeping a natural sleep, her expression tranquil.

'Much better, we think,' Susan's father said with a

smile, while her mother just smiled and her eyes filled with tears that seemed to be tears of gratitude, not trusting herself to speak.

'That's good.' Lisa smiled in turn. 'Take care.'

On the way out she spoke to a nurse. 'Is Susan Bowlder OK?'

'So far she's doing great. We seem to have got her in time. We have to monitor her pretty carefully, though. Can't relax too soon.'

From there she hurried up to Men's Surgical to see Carl Ottinger. At the elevators she met his daughter, Barb Hager, carrying a small suitcase.

'Hullo, Mrs Hager,' she said. 'You look as though you're about to take your father home.'

'Hi, it's great to see you!' The woman smiled. 'Yes, he's coming home. He's going to stay with me for a week, then he's going back to his place and we're all going to take turns, seeing that he's OK. I'm glad I met you because I wanted to let you know that I contacted my mother and that she's been in to see him every day since.'

'I'm glad to hear it. How did he take it?'

'Well, I could tell he felt a bit awkward with her at first. I think he felt guilty, you know, but I could tell he was really pleased too. It was funny, really, in a sad sort of way. He was trying so hard to be casual. It's going to work out OK.'

Mr Ottinger was sitting in a chair in his room, fully dressed in outdoor clothing. The change in his appearance was dramatic—there was colour in his cheeks, which had filled out, and his eyes were shining. A middle-aged woman was there, folding his pyjamas.

Barb Hager introduced her mother, then Lisa turned to Mr Ottinger. 'Just came to wish you well,' she said, extending her hand. 'You look really great.'

'I feel great,' he said. 'If I continue like this over the

next week or two I'm going to take a holiday, with plenty of sand, sun, and sea. . .or at least a lake.'

From the way his ex-wife smiled in the background Lisa would be surprised if she went with him. 'That's a good idea,' she said.

Feeling more uplifted, she went home, taking a different exit from the hospital, one of many—disguising her hair under a hat and wearing sun glasses. 'Two can play at this stalking game,' she said to herself firmly, with grim humour.

Saturday dawned warm and sunny, a good day to be off duty. When Lisa got up she dressed casually in loose pants and top. Emma was lying on her back, watching the door, when Lisa went in to her. She gave a sound of delight, waving her arms and legs vigorously.

'You cheeky little thing!' Lisa said, picking her up to cuddle her. 'You know I always come, don't you? Oh, what a spoiled girl you are, eh? Your every whim satisfied.'

Emma Kate grinned gummily, her large eyes shining with delight and health. Lisa felt her heart contracting with love. She had never guessed how much one could love a child, a different sort of love from the love of other family or from the love of a man. She knew she would give her life for her child. In return, her baby gave her unconditional adoration. She could see it in her eyes, an unspoken bond.

The morning went by quickly, filled with chores, laundry and cleaning. Later she would get out to enjoy the sunshine—maybe go for a walk, do a little gardening at the back of the house. She was looking forward to it.

There was a knock on the connecting door just before lunchtime and she unlocked it to admit her mother.

'I thought you might like me to take Emma for a walk in her stroller,' Mrs Stanton offered. 'It's such a gorgeous day. That would give you a chance to catch up with things.'

'That would be great. Thanks, Mum. Things have rather got piled up here.' She had rushed through the chores, wanting the place to look clean and bright.

When they were gone Lisa prepared a quick salad lunch. Before she could finish it the doorbell rang. She wasn't expecting anyone. Could it be Marcus? The question came instantly to her mind, fuelling her longing for him. Perhaps there was something he had to say to her in person, a new development.

Trying not to hurry, she saw the outline of a man through the panel of frosted glass in her front door, and her heart made a flip of anticipation. Maybe Marcus had decided to come—to surprise her. With a smile on her face, she flung the door open in expectation.

The smile froze, an awful parody of delight, as shock hit her like a physical blow. For a second or two her heart seemed to stop beating.

'Hello, Lisa,' the man said. 'May I come in?'

When she didn't reply, couldn't reply, he smiled. It was a smile that had no warmth or humour in it. 'Don't say you've actually forgotten my existence, Lisa,' he said, his voice a sarcastic drawl. 'Already? Who would have thought it?'

'Rich—' Lisa swallowed a hysterical lump in her throat, her voice catching. 'Richard! What. . .what are you doing here?'

'I'll explain, if you invite me in,' he drawled coldly. 'I always did know where your parents lived, you know. I figured you would still be here.'

Fighting for composure but recovering quickly, Lisa stood firmly in the doorway. 'What do you want?' she said bluntly. 'You never bothered to contact me in more than a year. I assumed you didn't want to. Well, Richard, I can honestly say now that the feeling's mutual.' How odd it was that she would once have flung herself into his arms.

Lisa swallowed to clear a nervous lump in her throat. Of their own accord, it seemed, her feelings had changed irrevocably. When she had seen that it was Richard she had at first felt shock, and not a pleasant shock. It had been coupled with something else that took her a few moments to analyse. It was a feeling of repulsion.

Richard had put on some weight in the intervening months since she had seen him. There was a jowly coarseness about him which had not previously been there, as though he overindulged himself in the good things of life.

There was no way that Lisa wanted to invite him in and let him know that she had a baby. At one time she would have wanted him to know—had desperately longed for his support, even though she had known in her heart of hearts that it would have been inadequate. Yet he was still the same Richard—dominating, powerful, overbearing and, yes, attractive in a rather heavy, swarthy sort of way, with a sexuality that promised much but didn't necessarily deliver.

'Don't play coy, Lisa,' he said roughly, his eyes going over her bare arms, then down to her feet and back again in a way that was familiar, as though he had a right of ownership. 'I understand you have a baby. My baby. Why the hell didn't you tell me you were pregnant?'

As she licked her dry lips Lisa felt as though all the blood was draining from the periphery of her body and rushing to the region of her heart. Don't say that he was going to make trouble for her, say that he had some sort of claim on Emma Kate! Please. . .

'And have you accuse me of becoming pregnant deliberately so that I could have some sort of permanent hold over you?' She laughed harshly. 'That is what you would have done, Richard. I know you only too well, you and your ego. If you're honest you'll admit it.'

Apparently, he was not about to be honest. 'I had a right to know that I had a child,' he said, looming large and threatening in the doorway, 'and I actually had to hear it from a third party. How do you think that made me feel? Like a first-class dummy, that's what!'

There was a note of exaggerated disgust in his voice, a tone that was familiar. She had forgotten how often he'd used that tone in the past to intimidate, or how often she had tried to overlook it. Now it jarred, a sickening memory. Yes, right from the very beginning he had been a bully. She had simply failed to recognize it for what it was until too late.

Not so long ago she would have flung herself at him. Now she could only stare, a sharp fear in her heart. 'A third party?'

'Dr Blair at University Hospital,' he said. 'I understand from him that you work there.'

'M-Marcus!' she said, stammering slightly in her surprise. 'How do you know Marcus?'

His eyes narrowed as he looked at her knowingly, not answering the question. 'So we're on first-name terms, are we?' There was a barely disguised sneer in his voice. 'You and. . .er. . .Marcus?'

'Yes,' she said bravely, her emotions chaotic. 'We're all on first-name terms in the emergency department. How do you know him? I. . .can't believe he would have told you without my permission.'

'Well, he did.' He smiled. 'I'd say you've got a thing going with our Dr Blair. Off with the old and on with the new, eh?'

'You were the one who wanted "off with the old", Richard. Or do you have a memory defect or something?' she said, lifting up her head to stare him full in the face.

'If you like, I can tell you what you said at the time—about how a year was the limit, maximum, that you could spend with any woman, that you got bored, had to have variety, or you'd go mad.'

'Did I say that?' he drawled, acting surprised.

'You know you did.' Lisa tried to keep any residual bitterness out of her voice. 'You didn't have anything against me, you said. It was just the way you were. And I just had to accept it. Maybe you would be that way with a child, too.'

He wore a suit with a shirt and tie and a light gabardine raincoat over the top of it, even though the day was warm, as though he had been somewhere formal. Seeing her perusal of his attire, he grinned slightly. 'I just came from a job interview, Lisa,' he said evenly. 'Dr Blair very kindly came to the hospital to interview me, even though he isn't on call this weekend.'

'What?' She was feeling slightly sick. Some months ago she might have welcomed this.

'Yes, that's right, Lisa. I'm going to be working in the emergency department at University Hospital for a period of three months before I take up a permanent position out west in the Yukon. Dr Blair. . .*Marcus*—' he gave the name a special emphasis '—has very kindly agreed to take me on as a sort of senior trainee.'

This couldn't be happening, Lisa thought frantically. Surely Marcus wouldn't take him on?

'He knew who I was, of course. After he told me I had a child I was able to put him straight about a few things,' Richard said, leaning nonchalantly against the doorframe.

'What do you mean?'

'I assured him that I certainly would have stood by you during your pregnancy and at the time of your delivery—had I known you were pregnant,' he said, with perfect calm and an apparent sincerity. Only she knew that it was false.

'You had no right to say that! I know otherwise,' she said, clenching her fists. 'The very thing I wanted to avoid was having you make me feel beholden to you, as though you were doing me a great big favour. That's why I didn't tell you. And I was right. I'm managing perfectly well.'

Without warning, Richard pushed past her into the hallway of her flat, pushing the door shut behind him at the same time.

'I'd like to see my baby,' he said.

'Why, Richard? What happened to the woman you left me for?' Lisa said, facing him. 'Or is she past history? It's well over the limit of a year since you started with her.'

He pursed his lips, his features hardening, so that Lisa took her assumption as a given. Without another word, he pushed past her and entered her sitting room. While she waited in the hall, feeling sick with a fear that he was trying to take her baby from her, she heard him go from room to room on the ground floor. Then, without looking at her, he mounted the small staircase to the second floor and the two bedrooms there.

'Where is she?' he demanded when he came down again.

'My mother's taken her out to visit friends,' she said calmly. 'They won't be back for some time. Don't think you can intimidate me, Richard.'

He made a sound of disgust as he went to the door. 'I intend to speak to my lawyer,' he said, turning to look at her, unsmiling, 'to find out exactly what my rights are.'

Lisa's mind moved like lightning over all the possibilities of future action on his part. One thing she had learned indelibly from living with him—he liked to win, liked to be in control.

'You do that, Richard, if it pleases you,' she said, knowing that overt resistance would only harden his resolve. 'I know you like to play power games. I don't think there is any court that would give you the child after your behaviour to me.'

'It will be a different story when they know I had no idea you were pregnant.'

'I don't think so. You left me. A reluctant man wouldn't make a good father,' she said. Knowing that he needed to appear to have won, in his own eyes as well as in hers, she added, 'By all means see her, if you wish. I wouldn't prevent you from doing that.'

Richard frowned. 'Like now,' he said sarcastically.

'I had no idea you were coming,' she said.

They faced each other for silent moments. 'I reckon we could make a go of it if we tried,' he said unexpectedly. 'Get together, I mean.' His expression belied his words. There was no warmth in his regard.

Intuitively, Lisa again knew what this was all about—control.

'I don't think so, Richard,' she said quietly, 'for several reasons. One of them is that I don't love you any more.'

As she said the words she knew, with a tremendous sense of relief, that they were true. The passion that she had felt for him had been like a fire which had burnt itself out, leaving only cold ashes. Without the underlying caring on his part to fuel the flames, they had died.

'Is that so?' he said dangerously. 'I shall tell my lawyer that I offered.'

'Don't threaten me, Richard. Don't pretend that you give a damn about me. The baby has a good home here, a loving home.'

'You're a single mother. I have money on my side. I will earn far more than you will ever earn,' he said.

Lisa shrugged. 'Do what you will,' she said. 'I'm past being intimidated by you. This is the nineteen nineties. I think you're about fifty years out of date.' Reaching past him, she released the latch on the front door and pointedly stood back for him to leave. 'Goodbye, Richard.'

'We'll see about that,' he said, as at last he left. Moments later she heard the engine of a car start up.

Leaning back against the wall, she felt weak with relief at his going, as well as some apprehension for the future. Was it possible that he could challenge her? She doubted it very much, yet she would get her father to speak to the family lawyer first thing on Monday morning. If she knew anything about Richard Decker he had little real interest in being a loving father to Emma Kate—the whole focus of his life was on himself.

Hard on the heels of that realization came another sharp anxiety, a sense of betrayal. Marcus had told Richard that she had a child. Then he had actually offered him a job where she worked. At the moment she could see no sense in any of it unless Marcus was completely disregarding her in this equation.

Distractedly she put a hand to her head and closed her eyes wearily. Life had been good over the past few weeks, apart from the nightmare of Charlene Damero with whom she felt she could cope. Now everything seemed to be slowly unravelling before her eyes. Guilt about Emma not having a father was now compounded by the awful realization that she, Lisa, couldn't accept Richard as Emma's father, even though he was the biological father. What a mess! Restlessly, she began to pace.

Making a quick decision, her mind now clearer, she went into the sitting room and left a note for her mother to say that she was borrowing her car and would be out for a short while. She intended to drive over to see Marcus and confront him face to face. There was no way she wanted to discuss this over the telephone. She wanted to see his expression, hear the tone of his voice.

There were several cars parked in the driveway of Marcus's house when, a short time later, Lisa brought her mother's small, compact car to a halt in the quiet street. The sight of them caused her resolve to waver for a few seconds. It seemed that he had visitors.

The man who answered the door was wearing a discreet uniform. Lisa wondered whether this was the butler that Marcus sometimes hired. Somehow the uniform didn't look quite right.

'Can I help you?' the man asked, as his eyes moved over her from head to toe, his manner not exactly welcoming.

'I'm a colleague of Dr Blair's,' she said. 'I'd like to see him, if I could.' It occurred to her then that he was a security guard.

A burst of laughter and the sound of conversation came to her from the direction of the drawing room which she knew from her previous visit. It looked as though she had interrupted a social gathering and she suddenly felt nervous, as though Marcus were an unknown quantity. But it was too late now to back off. She might as well go through with the confrontation, or whatever it turned out to be.

'Name?' the man said tersely, his gimlet eyes unsmilingly on her face.

'Lisa Stanton,' she said. Perhaps this man was from Ravi Davinsky's agency.

He spoke into a walkie-talkie, repeating her name to someone.

'Dr Blair will be out in a moment,' he said to her. It was clear that he was going to remain with her until Marcus appeared.

'Thank you,' she said.

To her relief, just when she was beginning to feel like an actress taking part in a third-rate movie, Marcus came out of the drawing room and walked rapidly towards them.

'Lisa.' He was obviously surprised, trying not to show it in front of the other man. 'It's nice to see you.' He nodded at the man with the walkie-talkie, who nodded in return and walked away.

'Not the butler, I guess,' Lisa commented dryly, looking after him.

'No. One of Ravi's men.' Marcus gave a small quirk of the mouth in that devastatingly rueful way that he had, which normally made her very susceptible to his charm. This time she tried hard to concentrate on the sense of betrayal that had brought her there in such a hurry.

'Come into the library,' he said, putting a hand under her elbow to usher her down a passage that led away from the main hall and the drawing room.

The library was a large, yet intimate-feeling room overlooking a garden, lined on three sides with bookcases in dark oak. A spacious desk and several chairs and smaller tables took up the centre of it. Marcus closed the heavy oak door and turned to her as she walked to the centre of the room on the thick carpet, her agitation evident.

'I can see from the expression on your face that you've come to see me about Dr Richard Decker,' he said, with an equanimity that contrasted strongly with Richard's confrontational manner earlier. Marcus looked at her quizzically, his eyebrows raised. In the casual blue denim jeans that he wore, with a checked shirt open at the neck, he managed to look effortlessly attractive in a very masculine way, quietly dominating as well as sophisticated.

Lisa dragged her eyes away from him, fighting for control, as she only now realized fully the task she had taken on in her decision to confront him. Seeing him again in his own setting, she knew forcefully that she had gradually, insidiously, become more emotionally involved with him.

'You. . .you seem to know me pretty well,' she said, with an uncharacteristic degree of sarcasm, surprised at the calmness of her own voice when the anger inside was building up to an explosive level.

'I doubt that,' he said, walking casually towards her and stopping a few feet away.

'Yes, I did come to talk to you about Richard,' she said with some asperity, trying not to be distracted by his attractiveness. 'I'm glad you got straight to the point.'

'Mmm,' he said. 'I'm sure you are going to do the same.' With his hands in his pockets, he stood regarding her.

'I realize that I have no say in the matter of whom you, as Head of Department, choose to hire.' She launched into her attack, honing her sarcasm—knowing that her face was tight with anger. 'It's just that I had been under the impression that, in a circumstance like this, you might have warned me first. I. . .I see now that I was expecting too much.'

He looked at her consideringly. 'He hasn't given me a chance, apparently,' he said reasonably. 'I just finished seeing him. . .' he glanced quickly at his wrist-watch '. . .less than two hours ago. He must have called you pretty quickly after that.'

'He came to the house,' Lisa said stiffly. 'Just presented himself at the front door.'

'I'm sorry to hear it. I had no idea he would do that,' Marcus said, frowning.

'You might have guessed he would do that, Dr Blair,' she said furiously, 'if you had given it any sort of thought. Why, Dr Blair? Why did you do it? And tell him that I had a baby? I don't understand,' she said, frustration in her voice. 'It's not as though we're short of doctors in the department. It's. . .it's almost like some sort of sick joke—at my expense.'

'You're right about what you said a moment ago—my decision to hire a doctor should not have to depend on the private considerations of one of the nurses,' he said.

Lisa gasped, trying to take in all the ramifications of what he was saying. 'You. . .you mean that you. . .that you didn't consider me at all?' She faced him, her hands clenched. 'When I am suffering inconvenience, not to mention danger, because a crazy woman has transferred her attentions to me because of you? I. . .I think that, at least, you could give me some reciprocal consideration.'

'Dr Decker telephoned me in the department yesterday afternoon after you had left. It just came out of the blue. I knew immediately who he was, of course. He has had a lot of experience in emergency work, and we could use an extra pair of hands over the summer months. I do happen to have the money in the departmental budget for an extra short-term salary,' Marcus said reasonably.

'But why him?' Lisa was almost sobbing with frustration. 'There must be any number of doctors known to you who would jump at the chance to work there.'

'Dr Decker told me he needed a temporary job for three months, before taking up a permanent position in the Yukon. I agreed to interview him today. I had to admit I was intrigued. It seemed like too good an opportunity to miss.' Marcus walked slowly over to her, closing the short distance between them, and Lisa felt herself back up until she felt the edge of the huge desk press against her body. Such was the tension that she felt she could scarcely breathe. 'Also, I did. . .um. . . I guess I saw it as a great opportunity. . .for you,'

'What do you mean—an opportunity for me?' She almost spat the words at him, an awful suspicion forming in her mind that perhaps he was trying to make her life so difficult that she left University Hospital. If she weren't there it was just possible that Miss Damero would be less fanatical. At the same time she chided herself that she was being paranoid.

'It will be the perfect opportunity for you to get together with him again—to have a father for your daughter,' he said. 'Or to decide, once and for all, what he means to you. Maybe to get him out of your system. . .if that's what you really want.'

'I know what I want, and it isn't that.' She just managed to get the words out. 'How dare you act in such a high-handed manner.'

'That wasn't what you gave me to believe when you last spoke to me of Richard Decker,' he reminded her, a harsh note in his voice now as he stared down at her broodingly. 'You weren't at all sure how you felt about him.'

'That was quite a while ago,' she said hotly, 'I don't want to work with him.'

'I'm afraid that's too bad,' Marcus said, his cool attitude contrasting with her hot-headed outburst. It seemed that all the pent-up distress of the past few months was coming out now. 'I have already hired him.'

'Well. . .you. . .stay out of my life,' Lisa found herself stammering, 'I. . .I'm grateful for what you did for me. Now just stay out. . .don't interfere.'

'As you wish,' he said quietly, moving abruptly away from her. He walked over to a window, his back to her.

'Do you want me to leave? Is that it?' she blurted. 'You want to make my life so uncomfortable that I'll go? That would simplify things for you.'

He turned to face her, his features stiff, expressionless. 'Of course not,' he said, 'but if that's what you have in mind who am I to persuade you otherwise?'

Tears blurred Lisa's vision as she stood momentarily at a loss.

'There was a tremendous loss of face for Dr Decker, not knowing you had given birth,' Marcus went on relentlessly, his dark, enigmatic eyes boring into her.

'Are you judging me? I lost more than "face", as you put it,' she said bitterly. 'He wouldn't make a good father or a good husband, and certainly not a good friend.'

'You obviously didn't think that when you got involved with him,' Marcus said harshly. 'And, for one who professes not to care for him any more, I'm frankly surprised that you're so. . .agitated.'

'That has nothing to do with you,' she said angrily. A thought came to her then, a moment of revelation. 'Just because you happen to be anti-woman, maybe because of what happened to you with Lydia Grenville, it doesn't mean that you are in a position to judge me. . .far from it.'

He grabbed her arm. He stared down at her with blazing eyes. 'What the hell do you know about her?'

'Not much.' She got the words out through gritted teeth. 'About as much, I expect, as you know about me and Richard Decker.' With that, she wrenched her arm out of his grip, backing away. 'Now. . .leave me alone, Marcus. . . Leave me alone.'

The last word came out on a sob, and then she ran away from him, pulled open the library door and walked swiftly down the passage to the front hall, keeping her face averted from the security guard who stood there. All the time she had the feeling that she hadn't said all that she'd wanted to say, hadn't said things very well. Now the opportunity was over.

Swiftly she ran down the front steps of the house to her car. In moments she was driving away, dimly aware that Marcus had come out to the steps—perhaps to stop her—but she didn't look back.

Near the end of the street she pulled the car over to the kerb, under the shade of a large tree, as tears blurred her vision, making driving dangerous. There was no one about on the quiet, residential street, which was more like a country road, so she let the tears fall. Miserably she knew that she was falling in love with Marcus Blair. What she felt for him was unlike her emotional involvement with Richard, which had centred around sexual attraction. With Marcus there was sexual attraction, all the more powerful because it had been unconsummated and so much more that had sprung from an unconditional caring.

That was why the uncharacteristic harshness of his response to her had been so hurtful. Maybe he was trying to break away from that sense of responsibility he had told her he had for her, and was now starting to push her away. There was no way that she wanted to leave the job she had come to love, yet she would if she had to. She wept then, her head bent forward to rest on the steering-wheel. For her and Marcus there could be no future.

CHAPTER NINE

SUMMER came with a vengeance, early and hot, with a humidity not usually present so early in the year. Lisa loved the heat after the bleakness of the long winter. In the evenings she played with Emma in the greening garden.

Work was more hectic than ever, falling into a well-ordered routine—as far as emergency work could ever be routine. She and Diane Crane felt that they were now old hands at the job and had also become firm friends, although Lisa hadn't confided her feelings about Marcus to her or anyone else. She did tell Diane that Richard was the father of her baby.

After she'd left Marcus's house that last time he'd telephoned her at home. As she rushed around at work she often thought of that perfunctory conversation and of how stilted she'd been, not wanting him to know how she mourned the loss of a sense of possibility between them that had tentatively bloomed like a delicate flower.

'When you've definitely made up your mind about Dr Decker,' Marcus had said, 'maybe we can be friends again.'

'Perhaps. . .' she'd said, not bothering to repeat that she had already made up her mind.

'Dr Decker has done a lot to sap your confidence as a woman, I think,' he'd said shrewdly. 'Am I right?'

'Yes, I expect you are.'

'You're still angry with me?'

'I'm afraid so,' she'd agreed. She had murmured a few more meaningless phrases and hung up, her heart heavy.

Since then she'd had no contact with him over the past

two weeks, other than in his capacity as a team member. It was almost as though he was standing back, giving her a mental push in the direction of Richard Decker who'd started work a few days after she'd confronted him. Working with Richard, plus the tension between herself and Marcus, was taking its toll on her. Consequently, she welcomed major accidents, the 'high' of being challenged to the limit, which had the effect of wiping all else from her mind.

Richard had always been a good, skilled doctor. Now he proved himself a useful member of the team. By accident, or deliberate machinations on someone's part, Lisa seldom found herself working alone with Richard. By the same token, although she worked a lot with Marcus they were almost always surrounded by others.

'Lisa, I want to see you in my office in five minutes,' Marcus said to her at the end of one very busy morning, accosting her in the main corridor of the stretcher section of the department. He scarcely paused in his stride as he went past her in the opposite direction so that anyone who might have observed them wouldn't have noticed that he'd spoken to her.

Wracking her brains to think of something she might have done wrong, she finished what she was doing before she headed towards his office. These days it seemed to her that he was becoming more and more like a stranger to her. Very pointedly, he seemed to be avoiding her. Maybe, she told herself frantically, he was giving her a chance to become reconciled with Richard. That, she knew now, could never happen. Too much water had gone under the proverbial bridge.

Marcus was already in his office, with the door open, when she got there.

'Come in,' he said when he saw her. As soon as she entered he shut the door firmly. He looked, she saw, as strained and pale as she was herself—and as tired. His hair, longish these days, looked as though he had impatiently raked a hand through it many times. There was a plate of sandwiches in the room and the usual coffee.

'Have you had lunch?' he asked.

'Um. . .no. I haven't eaten since breakfast at about six this morning,' she said.

'Help yourself to sandwiches.'

'Thank you.' She picked one up and bit into it, feeling faint from hunger.

'Perhaps you'd like some coffee?' he said.

'Well. . .perhaps just a very quick one, please,' she said. In fact, she was desperate for coffee. His presence seemed to fill the entire room so that she felt suffocated. 'Is there something in particular you have to say to me, Dr Blair? I do have to get back. As I'm part time I don't get more than fifteen minutes' break—not a proper lunch-break.'

'Of course,' he said. Abruptly he turned from her to pour them both coffee. 'I wanted to ask you whether Dr Decker has done anything about getting legal access to your baby.' He placed the full cups on the desk between them.

Swallowing the mouthful of sandwich, Lisa collected her thoughts quickly as he looked at her unsmilingly.

'I. . .haven't actually asked him,' she said hurriedly, 'and he hasn't said anything. Our lawyer said that he would have to apply to the courts for access to her.'

'I see. Do you suppose he will?'

'Knowing him as I do, I think he would have to at least make a gesture,' she said, bending her head. She was unwilling to meet his brooding eyes, wanting him to be the way he had been before. 'I'm actually surprised that he hasn't done anything yet. I doubt very much that he actually wants a baby. . .'

'Will you let me know if he does? I would like to know.'

'Why, Dr Blair?' she asked challengingly. 'That inappropriate sense of responsibility again?'

'You could say that,' he murmured, giving Lisa the impression that he had really wanted to ask about herself and Richard and whether they were resolving any differences.

'We are not about to get married. Dr Decker and I have been avoiding each other as much as possible,' she said, determined to bring any supposition out into the open. 'By mutual, unspoken consent. He has a new girlfriend. She meets him sometimes in the hospital lobby. . . I've seen them several times.' At least, she had seen him meet a woman and had made the assumption about her relationship to Richard. 'Actually, I'm relieved that he has her.'

'I see.' Marcus handed her a cup of coffee. 'The other thing,' he said, moving restlessly around the room, 'is that Miss Damero has been spotted, and warned off, several times in the vicinity of the hospital over the past two weeks—both by Ravi's men and the hospital security people—near the entrances. I wanted to warn you to be careful, Lisa. Things seem to be hotting up. She may be planning something.'

'I am careful,' Lisa said. 'I take a different exit every day.'

'Good,' he said tensely. 'What burns me up is that there's little we can do about her until she actually does something definite—makes a move. After all, a hospital is public property, even though no one is normally here without legitimate reasons.'

'I know how to be careful,' she said stiffly. 'Is there anything else you wanted to see me about?' Inside, she felt like weeping.

'No. . .' He had hesitated before the word. Intuitively she knew that he was not as indifferent to her personally as he would like her, and himself, to believe.

Mercifully, the telephone on his desk rang and as he answered it Lisa drained her coffee cup, then helped herself to another sandwich and a paper napkin. She left his office, knowing she was running away. She felt even less sure about anything.

When she was in the triage station later, entering data into the computer prior to going off duty, she looked up to see Richard in the lobby talking to his 'girlfriend'. Without consciously forming a definite plan, she headed out to accost him. The tension of not knowing what his intentions were with regard to Emma Kate was getting to her in a serious way.

Richard looked big and dominating, like a professional rugby player, his muscles rippling beneath the thin cotton of his green scrubsuit. It was this overt masculinity which had attracted her initially. Now she found it slightly repugnant, an over-stated case that didn't really mean much.

'Hullo, Richard,' she said, with an acknowledging nod to his companion. 'I was. . .um. . .wondering if you would like to see Emma Kate this next weekend? Or maybe you would like to take her for the weekend? Then you could really get to know her.'

With that, she looked from one to the other, as though including his companion in the invitation. All the time she felt sick with worry in case he actually took up the offer. It was a gamble that she had to take—to call his bluff, if that was what it was. She was banking on an educated guess that he didn't really want a baby but simply wanted to throw his weight about, to dominate.

Richard straightened from the intimate, slouching stance which had inclined him towards the other woman. A look of what Lisa took to be muted, stupefied horror came over his face, and a slow, dark red flush moved up from his neck to suffuse his cheeks.

The woman looked enquiringly from one to the other, frowning. 'And who,' she said chirpily, 'is Emma Kate? Do you share a stray cat or something?'

Lisa could almost have laughed, if there hadn't been so much that was serious hanging on his reply. She forced herself to continue. 'Emma Kate is my baby,' Lisa said, saying each word slowly and clearly. If Richard was really serious about having a baby he would obviously have to inform the woman in his life. A sense of relief came over her as it was clear that he hadn't told this particular woman.

'She's also Richard's baby,' she added quietly but firmly. 'Did he not tell you that? Frankly, I'm surprised. You see, he's claimed that he would like to have legal access to her.'

It wasn't possible to say which one of the two people in front of her looked the more stunned. Richard's face was almost thunderous with anger, while the woman looked so taken aback that Lisa found it in her heart to feel sorry for her.

'Well?' Lisa said, pressing her advantage, even though her heart was thudding with nervousness. 'I'm rather fed up with all the emotional blackmail, Richard. Please make up your mind one way or the other so that I can instruct my lawyer accordingly.'

With that, she turned on her heel and walked away, just as a nurse approached calling, 'Oh, Dr Decker, you're needed in—' She didn't hang about to hear more. Richard hadn't uttered a single word.

A curious kind of elation buoyed her up as she made her way to the locker room to change to go home. Perhaps now she would get some answers so she could sort out her life. Never would she forget the resounding silence from Richard after he had made love to her that last time, after implying that there could be some sort of future for them. A silence that had lasted for over a year. . . That silence had told her much.

Perhaps it was just as well that the following week was extremely busy at work. With the coming of summer a number of medical students had come to work in the emergency department for a few weeks to get some clinical experience, thus adding to the total number of staff. For Lisa it meant that she was seldom alone with either Marcus or Richard. Life for Marcus was busier than ever as he planned training programmes for the students.

On a few occasions Lisa saw Richard looking at her darkly, yet he could say nothing to her that wasn't directly related to the job in hand. So far he hadn't said anything about Emma Kate, and Lisa felt her spirits lifting and began to hope that perhaps he was backing off.

'Dr Decker sure has an eye for a pretty face, and everything else that goes with it,' Diane Crane said cheerfully to Lisa one morning. 'The sort of guy who always wants to keep his options open.'

'Diagnosis perfect!' Lisa smiled at her. 'Your frankness is refreshing, Diane.'

'Maybe he'll wake up one day, when he's about forty, and realize that he hasn't got any more options and that women only want him for his money—assuming that he has some.'

'I think you're right on there, Diane,' Lisa found herself laughing. 'See. . .I can even laugh about it!'

'Great! Keep on laughing, girl!' Diane replied. 'This is going to be one of those days, I can tell. Look at all those people coming through the doors. The waiting room's pretty full already.'

The morning went by in a mad rush of work. When Lisa finally got to look at her wrist-watch she saw that she only had two hours of work left. As she hurried through the lobby to check at the triage station she was brought up short by the sight of Ravi Davinsky coming through the central glass doors to the department. Although he wore dark glasses and had discarded his suit and gabardine raincoat for more seasonal attire she would have recognized him anywhere, if only by his oily curls that spilled boyishly over his high forehead.

Equally, he recognized her and made a beeline for her.

'Hi, there, Miss Stanton,' he hailed her. 'Great to see you.' He extended a hand, gripping hers in a fulsome greeting. 'Just the person I was hoping to see. Is Marcus around? I would like to see the two of you together, if I can.'

'We'll try his office,' Lisa offered, and led the way, dodging around people who were coming in and going out. 'Is anything up?'

'Could be,' Ravi said, panting a little with effort, as though he had been running.

Marcus was in his office with three medical students when they got there. Excusing himself, he came out into the corridor to talk to them. 'What's up?' he said.

'My men have lost sight of Miss Damero,' Ravi said. 'She's not at her place of work and not on vacation—we checked. Not in her apartment—we checked that. She isn't in her usual haunts—cafés and so on, where she goes for relaxation.'

'Damn!' Marcus said.

'She's been out of sight for twenty-four hours,' Ravi said, taking off his sunglasses to reveal tired eyes. 'That could mean that she's up to something.'

'Like what?' Lisa asked.

'She could have checked into a hotel under a false name. People like her have any number of names. . .with stolen IDs to back them up. My guess is that she's done just that. Most likely, she's going around in disguise.' He took out a handkerchief to wipe sweat from his forehead. 'I came here to ask you to be extra careful. Next, I've got an appointment with the hospital security people.'

Marcus looked at his watch. 'Could one of you guys escort Miss Stanton home when it's time for her to leave here?'

'Sure,' Ravi said obligingly.

'Lisa, you'd better call your mother,' Marcus said tiredly, his face tense. 'Advise her not to take the baby out. I wouldn't put it past Miss Damero to try something there.'

'Quite right,' Ravi agreed. 'She may be gearing up for the grand finale. What we have to do is be one step ahead of her, if we can.'

Lisa nodded, her throat tight with fear.

'I'll be back here shortly,' Ravi said, 'after I've spoken to Security. I'll let you know what they say.'

'Right,' Marcus said. He and Lisa stood together, watching the detective stride away from them down the corridor. 'Lisa, I'm going to talk to Sadie Drummond again about this and ask her to keep you away from the front lobby. I'll also tell Elsa Graham to give you work back here in the resuscitation rooms. Hopefully, if Miss Damero comes in here we'll spot her before she sees us. Stay back here.' The expression on his face was unreadable as he looked at her, his mouth compressed, yet she imagined that his gaze softened a little as his eyes met hers.

'OK,' she said.

'Once again, I'm more sorry than I can possibly say that you've got dragged into this madness.' For once the great strain of the situation showed clearly on his face. 'I just hope that the "grand finale", as Ravi put it, will come soon—as long as no one gets hurt in the process. I'm getting pretty sick of this.'

'I can look after myself,' she said, more bravely than she felt, looking away from him down the corridor. A quiet resolve had formed in her a long time ago. 'You take care as well.'

'Well. . .I have to get back to my students,' Marcus said quietly. 'Ask Elsa Graham to come to my office, please. Take care.' There was an unbearable tension between them that both propelled her towards him and made her want to get away at the same time—as though if she stayed in his presence for more than a few moments she would let him see the confused love that was growing in her.

'Yes.' Lisa went quickly through the double doors into the room which she knew needed to be cleared up and prepared for another case. She could see that the whole place was in a shambles.

'Dr Blair said I'm to help you clear up here,' she said to Elsa Graham, 'and he wants to see you now in his office.'

'OK,' Elsa said. 'Set this place up with the usual packs, please, Lisa. With the rate things are going today, we're going to need it pronto.'

When Elsa had gone out Lisa set to work quickly and methodically, clearing and setting up the room. There was a central operating table, an anaesthetic machine and the usual accoutrements. She found the familiar work soothing, yet she couldn't suppress a sharp premonition. There had been something urgent about Ravi Davinsky's concern. . .

Marie, the nurse whom Lisa avoided if she could because she was bad-tempered and unfriendly, poked her head round the door.

'Is this room free?' she asked abruptly. 'We've got some cases over the other side, things that need suturing, that may have to come over here because we're running out of space there. We've got a minor head injury, a woman with a badly lacerated hand and a few other borderline serious cases.' There was a belligerent note in her voice, as though she were challenging Lisa to deny her space.

'As you can see, this room isn't ready yet,' Lisa said, waving her arm to encompass the disorder of the room, 'but I'm pretty sure that rooms one and two are OK. Try those.'

Without another word, Marie left the room. Sighing, Lisa went back to her tasks, her mind running ahead to decide on the equipment that she would need to collect. Elsa had already wheeled a small trolley into the room, piled up with the necessary sterile packs which were wrapped in green cotton drapes and tied up with string like parcels.

After a few moments Lisa became aware that someone else had put a head around the door. Looking up from where she had been covering the operating table with a clean green cotton sheet, she saw a woman with short dark hair and glasses staring at her.

'Hi,' Lisa said, pausing in her task, 'can I help you?'

The woman, the top half of her body around the door, had a hand held up against her chest, and Lisa could see that the hand was covered with a blood-soaked towel wrapped tightly around it.

'I was told to come in here,' the woman whispered. 'I've cut my hand. I was told it needs stitches.'

'Oh, not in here,' Lisa said kindly. 'That will be next door in room two.' She pointed in the direction of the other resuscitation room. 'Just go in there. Someone will be with you.'

'Thank you,' the woman whispered.

Lisa tucked the sheet in neatly around the operating table, thinking it a little odd that a patient with a badly cut hand would be sent over here by herself from the other side of the department. Usually a nurse would accompany her and show her exactly where she had to go. There was always the danger that a bleeding patient might faint, even if they weren't losing much blood. There was always shock, with any sort of injury, which would lower the blood pressure.

Just as Lisa resolved to check up to see if the injured woman had been received by a nurse in the room next door she became aware that she wasn't alone. Even before she turned to face the door there was an odd sense of a prickling awareness that she was being observed.

Looking over her shoulder, with a primitive instinct of impending danger, she saw the woman with the injured hand standing quietly in the room a few feet away from the door. Lisa hadn't heard her come back in.

With an odd, almost clinical detachment Lisa's eyes fell to the floor at the woman's feet. The blood-soaked towel was on the floor, discarded. As Lisa's heart gave a sickening lurch of recognition, not so much from the woman's face as from what she held in her hand, she turned slowly so that her back was to the operating table and she could slide her hand along the edge of it right to the end. She edged away, not taking her eyes off the face with the glasses, surrounded as it was by the short, unfamiliar dark hair.

In the woman's right hand—the injured hand, from which blood was dripping from a visible cut in the fleshy part of the palm—was a knife. It was a large knife, eight or nine inches long, with a blade that tapered to a sharp point. The woman held it in the stabbing position, as though all she had to do was raise it and bring it down.

For a few seconds, which seemed to stretch like long minutes, Lisa felt a paralysis—a brief lassitude—come over her, as though her brain was gathering its resources, before telling her what to do.

Then the adrenalin started to flow—the body chemical responsible for flight and fight. She felt it, like a surge of power through her body, together with a sick knowledge that this was the 'grand finale' that Ravi Davinsky had been talking about.

Behind the glasses the cold eyes stared out at her. The lips, devoid of make-up now, were twisted in a familiar grimace of hate.

'Miss Damero, we've been waiting for you,' Lisa said, wondering how her own voice could sound so calm when her heart was thudding with something like terror. At the same time her thoughts were becoming as clear as crystal. 'This place is full of security men and police.'

All was evident now, from the obviously self-inflicted hand wound to the dark wig and the glasses.

Miss Damero laughed derisively. 'I'm going to kill you,' she said, her voice curiously flat, her eyes staring.

Perhaps she was on drugs, Lisa thought frantically as she reached behind her to grip the metal edges of the operating table, her mind searching for a plan of self-defence.

Out of the corner of her eye she could see the small trolley, piled high with the sterile packs, near the bottom end of the operating table. At the top end of that table was the anaesthetic machine which held several potential weapons that could be used in a pinch—a laryngoscope, McGill's endotracheal forceps, scissors, various artery forceps—none of them any match for a knife. Anyway, the machine was too far away from her to reach now and too close to Miss Damero, who stood between her and the door. It would have to be the packs. . .

On the wall, beyond the bottom end of the operating table, was the red emergency button, projecting three inches from the wall, that could be pushed in to summon help. Lisa refrained from actually looking at it. It was used in cases of severe haemorrhage, cardiac arrest, respiratory arrest or any other sort of emergency. If she could get to that a whole team would respond within seconds.

Not taking her eyes off Miss Damero, she inched towards it.

'I'm going to kill you,' the woman said again. Slowly, like an animal stalking its prey, she advanced silently two steps towards Lisa. The knife in her hand was raised, held close to her body just above waist level.

'You're going to have your work cut out for you,' Lisa said, taunting her, aware of the ghastly pun. 'I don't kill easy.' I have a baby to live for, she might have added.

As Charlene Damero ran towards her, the knife raised to strike, Lisa supported her weight on both her arms on the operating table behind her. When the woman was within kicking distance she leaned back on the table to a semi-sitting position, drawing up her knees, with the weight of her body against the table. Then she kicked out with both feet and caught the other woman in the midriff region as hard as she could. At the same time she screamed involuntarily, a scream of pure terror.

Charlene Damero doubled up in pain, her face contorting, before she let loose a string of profanities and came at Lisa again. 'I know Marcus has been sleeping with you,' she snarled. 'I've been watching your place. He won't be doing it again. . .because you're going to be dead.'

Quickly, in desperation, not taking her eyes off the other woman as she grappled her with her right hand, Lisa groped sideways with her left hand to the pile of sterile packs. She had noticed several small gown packs there before. Each one contained four folded gowns, packed tight, and four hand towels, the whole making a compact parcel that was surprisingly heavy.

With her hand flailing sideways as they rocked back and forth in a macabre wrestling match—the woman's free hand grabbing her hair—Lisa frantically reached for one of those packs and almost sobbed with relief when her hand encountered it. Getting the fingers of her hand under the string that held it together, she put all her body weight on her right foot and swung the pack at Miss Damero's head and neck, allowing her weight to carry it forward. With a satisfying thud it struck home and the woman staggered sideways.

At the same time the hand with the knife slashed at Lisa as she loosened her grip on the arm that held it. She felt it cutting her left arm above the elbow. Again she screamed, a shrill, piercing sound of desperation.

'Lisa! Lisa!' An anguished male voice called her name. Not daring to take her eyes off Miss Damero, she saw on the periphery of her vision a white-coated figure coming towards them.

'Lisa. . . For God's sake, get back. . . Get back. . .out of the way!' he was shouting at the top of his voice.

'Marcus. . .look out. . .look out. . . She has a knife!' Lisa screamed the words as Marcus came up to them at a run and grabbed Miss Damero, gripping both her arms.

'Drop that knife!' she heard him bellow furiously. 'Drop it right now!'

Instinctively, Lisa lunged towards the emergency button and with all her strength smashed it into the wall as far as it would go, aware that she was half sobbing, half panting. She also noted that, curiously, her white uniform was red with blood all down the front; she hadn't noticed that before. From somewhere outside in the corridor the sharp, shrill sound of an emergency siren filled her ears.

'Thank God!' She sobbed the words, turning frantically to help Marcus.

'I'll kill you, Marcus,' Miss Damero was shouting shrilly, her face red with the effort of struggling with him. 'If I can't have you no one else will.'

'That's a rather hackneyed line,' Marcus shouted with grim humour as he struggled. 'You might have thought of something more original to justify all this, Miss Damero.'

As Lisa watched Marcus put a foot between Miss Damero's feet and tripped her up and at the same time he succeeded in wresting the knife from her grasp. When it hit the floor he kicked it savagely so that it skittered into a far corner of the room.

Suddenly the room was full of people. Ravi Davinsky was there, as were the hospital security people, Dr Nathan Hanks—with several of the interns—Richard Decker, Sadie Drummond and Elsa Graham. Within seconds, the security personnel were wrestling with Miss Damero on the floor. One of them held a strait-jacket.

'What the hell's going on, Marcus?' Dr Hanks said, his intelligent, normally good-humoured face creased in concern as he took in the mad scene. For once, Sadie Drummond seemed temporarily struck dumb.

Marcus's eyes searched for Lisa in the crowded room. He pushed his way towards her and enclosed her in his arms. 'A crazy woman with a knife,' he said tersely. 'Lisa's been stabbed. Help me get her onto a stretcher, Nathan. Quick, man!'

'All this blood. . .' Lisa said, looking down at her uniform.

'Yes. . . Hell,' Marcus murmured, anguish in his voice as he pressed her against him, 'Take it easy, honey.'

'I'm all right,' she said, even as she was aware that she was shivering with shock.

'No, you're not,' he said. 'You've been cut, quite deep by the look of it, on the upper arm.'

Several of the doctors lifted her onto a stretcher. Richard, pale-faced, was one of them. 'Are you OK?' he said. Lisa nodded.

In the centre of the room a struggle was going on with the demented woman as she fought the security men, kicking, screaming and swearing in as foul a language as anyone there had heard.

'Here's a tourniquet,' Dr Hanks's calm voice said, and Lisa felt his hands on her arm. 'Then we'll take a look at the extent of the damage.'

'Richard,' Marcus said, 'would you take charge of the department for me while I get all this sorted out?'

'Sure. . .'

'Marcus,' Lisa said, looking up at him as he bent over her, 'are you all right?'

'Never better,' he said grimly, as he helped Nathan ease her uniform aside to expose the stab wound on her upper arm. 'At least this is the end of Miss Damero as far as we're concerned.'

'But you're bleeding, Marcus,' she insisted frantically. 'There's blood all over you.'

'Most of it's yours,' he said. 'What's a little blood in an emergency department, anyway? It's you I'm worried about.'

'I. . .think it's just a surface cut,' she said, watching Nathan and Marcus exchange glances. 'Are you sure you're all right?'

'Yes, quite sure.' Although his voice was terse, there was an underlying note of unaccustomed anxiety in his voice as he and Dr Hanks stopped the flow of blood, pressing a thick dressing to the wound.

'Looks like an artery,' Dr Hanks muttered as the two doctors conferred with each other.

'Yes,' Marcus agreed. 'Lisa, we're going to get one of the peripheral vascular surgeons to see you. OK? It looks as though that knife got the artery. He'll clamp it off for us, then do a bit of stitching.'

'All right,' she said. 'I. . .I don't want to look at it.'

'We'll wheel you into the next room.' Sadie Drummond

was there beside them. 'We need to get away from this madhouse.'

In a quiet adjoining room Marcus bent over her and put more pressure on the bleeding point, while Sadie Drummond moved about purposefully within the scope of Lisa's peripheral vision, getting equipment together for the vascular surgeon who was on his way.

'This feels like the re-run of an old movie,' Lisa said tiredly, in an attempt at humour, looking up at Marcus as he covered her with another blanket. She was shivering with shock. 'Here I am flat on my back again, with you administering to my needs.'

'Maybe that's my destiny,' he quipped. 'I'm indebted to you now—to the sacrifice you made.'

'No, you're not. . . Now we're quits,' she said quietly, wincing with pain as Dr Hanks put more pressure on her arm. 'I don't owe you anything any more. . .' Realizing that what she said was true, she closed her eyes with a sense of relief and shut out his tired, strained face. It was almost worth being stabbed to know that the sense of indebtedness she'd felt towards Marcus could be put into perspective.

'Is the arm hurting?' Marcus asked.

'Yes. I can feel it now.' In truth, the whole arm was throbbing painfully, a sharp pain that was increasing. 'I didn't notice it much at the time.'

'I'll put up an IV and give you some Demerol for the pain.'

People were going in and out of the room. Lisa didn't bother to look around her, the throbbing in her arm taking over her awareness. . .and the relief that both she and Marcus were safe.

As Marcus bent close to her to insert the cannula into a vein in her hand for the IV line she looked at him, wanting so much to put her good arm around his neck and pull him close to her—feel his cheek against hers. When their eyes met he must have read something of her anguish in hers for he touched her face briefly in a gentle caressing gesture which no one else could have interpreted as anything out of the ordinary.

'When all this is finally over we'll go out for a drink together. Hmm?' he said quietly.

Lisa nodded, feeling a tightness of emotion in her throat and the threat of tears in her eyes.

'The vascular guy's here,' Nathan Hanks called from the doorway.

'He may want to take her to the main operating room,' Marcus said quietly to Dr Hanks.

Lisa could hear them conferring with the vascular surgeon just inside the door, telling him what had happened. Then she felt gentle fingers lifting the dressing on her arm. After a short silence the surgeon said, 'I want to take you to the main operating room, Miss Stanton. I would rather not deal with this in the emergency department because you may need a general anaesthetic. When did you last have anything to eat or drink?'

The hot summer sun was muted, filtered through leaves of elm and maple trees which grew near the park bench where Lisa sat. The grass in the small park had recently been mown and it gave off that characteristic scent that depicted the lazy days of summer so well. Emma Kate was in her pram under a sunshade, fast asleep. She lay on her back with her arms flung out to the sides and her head turned towards Lisa, her bare feet protruding from beneath the soft white cotton dress which was sprigged with a motif of pale blue flowers.

As Lisa watched her, squinting lazily against the sun, she felt her heart swell with love and pride—and a thankfulness that she was privileged to be the mother of this beautiful child who could so easily have died. She didn't feel anything for Richard any more other than a vague, distant sadness. Maybe he had actually done her a favour in a way by giving her this child.

It had all been worth it—all the anxiety and the pain, the fear for the future—every minute of it. As she looked at the downy hair, resting in soft curls on her daughter's forehead, and the long, dark lashes that fanned her plump cheeks Lisa knew a deep contentment. Yet underneath her contentment was a sense of loss, almost a mourning, and a sense of waiting for something to happen.

She had been off work for three weeks, after having her arm stitched up. The wound was well healed now and she was to go back to work after another week. She had stayed in hospital for a day after the minor operation, during which time all her colleagues with whom she was close had come to see her. Marcus had come—had been there when she'd come round from the anaesthetic. Groggy from the drugs, she had felt him kiss her. . .or thought she had. Then after she had gone home she hadn't seen him again.

That absence niggled now, a sense of disappointment and longing, even as she told herself again and again that there was no reason now for them to have any sort of personal contact outside work. Now that Miss Damero was in custody they had no reason to see each other, although there would be a court case at some point in the future.

He had telephoned, of course, sometimes more than once a day, during the first week. But she missed him, longed for him with an intensity that was like a physical ache. Others had called, too—like Sadie Drummond, whose conversation still echoed in Lisa's brain. Not for one moment could she get that out of her mind.

'Dr Blair was really great, wasn't he?' Sadie had

enthused. 'We'd sure miss him if he went to Africa.'

'Africa?' Lisa had said weakly.

'Yeah. That organization. . .what is it? International Physicians? They want him to go to Rwanda, or Burundi or some such place. He's considering it. I sure hope he doesn't go. . .' Sadie had gone on at great length, while Lisa had stopped hearing what she was saying. She'd only been able to think of her own impending loss.

She knew that Marcus had come to mean so much to her—that she loved him. A life without him in it somewhere would be incomplete. With a sigh, a feeling of restlessness, she closed her eyes and leaned her head back against the trunk of a tree behind the bench. Marcus had shown her something of what a mature relationship between two people could be like. Thoughts of him seemed to fill her whole being. . .

Something made her look up—along the path towards the entrance to the park. A man was coming towards her—a tall man, who walked easily and was wearing a lightweight business suit with a striped shirt and tie. Lisa blinked, wondering if the heat was playing tricks with her vision—if she was seeing a mirage—or whether from her intense longing she had conjured up an apparition that would dissipate if she looked at it too hard. There was something about his casual elegance, the way he walked, that was familiar. Then her heart gave a lurch of recognition. It *was* Marcus. In a way she wasn't surprised—it was as though she had sensed his nearness.

What would he be doing here, in this park? She asked herself the question, hardly daring to hope that he had come to see her. Yet he was walking in her direction, coming to where she sat a little off the path. As he left the path and stepped onto the grass her heart began to beat like a wild thing.

'Hi,' he said, coming up to her. 'Your mother said you

would be here. I came to find you.' How dear he was! Lisa wanted to jump up and fling her arms around his neck. Instead, she just sat there, staring at him as if he were an apparition. His hair was windblown, his tie loose.

'Aren't you going to say anything?' He smiled down at her in a way that would have melted the resistance of a stone, and she was far from that. 'May I sit down?'

'I. . . Yes, please do,' she said, stammering a little like an actress fluffing her lines. 'Why. . .why have you come to find me?'

When he was seated next to her his eyes went over her as though he wanted to renew his vision of her. 'I wanted to see you,' he said softly, 'and I thought it was time we had that drink.' The lines at the corners of his eyes crinkled up when he smiled.

'To. . .er. . .say goodbye?' she blurted, very conscious of his nearness. 'I understand you're going to Africa.'

'No. They wanted me to go. I refused.' To her relief, he turned his attention to Emma Kate who looked so adorable, oblivious to the world. Otherwise he would have seen how vulnerable she was as she felt some of the tension drain from her. 'It's too soon after starting my new post as Head of Department. There are other reasons as well.'

'Oh. . .'

A ethereal kind of silence surrounded them.

'It's nice to see you, Lisa,' he said after a while.

'Yes,' she agreed. 'I mean. . .it's nice for me to see you as well.'

'I've missed you,' he said, leaning back against the wooden bench and stretching out his long legs.

'Mmm. . . I've missed you,' she said.

'Another reason I came. . . Richard Decker has agreed not to press for any sort of legal custody. Your confrontation seems to have helped him to make up his mind,' Marcus said slowly, gazing out over the sun-dappled park and allowing her time to sort out her emotions. 'It appears that he intends to take his latest girlfriend with him to the Yukon. He did concede that he might want to see Emma Kate from time to time.'

'I see. That's a relief,' Lisa said. 'Thank you for conveying the news. Thank you for coming.'

'My pleasure. Do you care at all that he's finally going?' There was a tenseness about him and he did not look at her.

'No. It's finished,' she said truthfully. 'I feel wonderfully free.' What about you? she wanted to say. You must know that I love you—you must! Instead, she sat immobile. 'Why did you hire him, Marcus?'

'I wanted to precipitate something. I wanted you to confront the issue. And I wanted to see if I cared,' he said tensely. 'Although I couldn't admit that at the time—not to myself, not to you.'

'Did you care?' she whispered.

'Yes, like hell. Lisa. . .' Then his arm was along the back of the bench and his fingers on the sensitive skin of her neck, drawing her towards him, his eyes on her mouth.

'Marcus. . .' She whispered his name, allowing herself to move to him. Please kiss me, she wanted to say. Instead, she parted her lips to receive him, closing her eyes.

When his mouth at last came down on hers she sighed against him, letting her body go into his arms. All her senses were heightened. She heard the sound of the breeze in the trees, felt the sun caress her skin and smelt the scent of grass mingling with his tantalizing cologne. Then her arms were around his neck, her hand in his hair, pulling him to her as though she could never let him go.

They were oblivious to the surrounding world as the kiss went on an on, the touch of him like molten fire running through her veins, every part of her totally aware of him. He crushed her to him, kissing her with an abandon to match her own as he made a primitive sound of longing deep in his throat. Then she knew that the long wait was over, and that he wanted her as much as she wanted him.

When at last he took his mouth from hers, he kissed her neck and murmured words of love in her ear. 'Knowing you has made me realize what really matters. . .to get my priorities sorted out. . .' he murmured, kissing the lobe of her ear.

Convulsively she kissed him, teasing his lips with hers. 'Marcus, I'm so glad you came to find me.'

He wrapped his arms round her tightly. 'When you were going to have your baby,' he said huskily, 'I found myself wishing that you were mine—that you were my wife, that it was my baby you were having. It was a revelation to me, perhaps because it was forced upon me in such a dramatic way—because I was part of it. I discovered what it really means to care about someone in an intimate way, instead of usually being on the outside of things. No other woman has meant that to me.'

'Oh, Marcus.' She breathed his name softly, putting her head on his shoulder. Their hands clasped.

'Then, when I saw Emma Kate,' he continued, 'I knew I wanted her to be mine. . .'

'You were wonderful. . . I. . .I wish I had been your wife,' she said wistfully.

'Darling. . .' He kissed her hungrily, the sexual tension seeming to crackle between them like a living thing. 'It's been such a long time.'

'I love you, Marcus. . . You must know that.' At last she could say those words, knowing he was ready to receive them. A wariness in him had gone.

'You've helped me achieve a balance,' he said, cupping her face in his hands. 'To look at my life in a different way. I need a wife, I need children. Not anyone—you!' He kissed her again. 'What I'm trying to say is that I love you, too.'

'I'm so happy.' She smiled up at him. 'And I know I've finally grown up.'

'I solemnly promise I'll be good to you, and for you.'

'I know you will. I'm ready to make the same promise.'

Marcus nuzzled her hair, holding her close. 'I want to make love to you and I want to marry you. . .not necessarily in that order, but preferably so. Please.' There was laughter in his voice, to which Lisa found herself responding with a wild leap of joy. 'Should I kneel at your feet?'

'Not necessary, Dr Blair,' she teased as she laughed up at him, 'Yes. . .yes to both requests. Come home with me, with us. Stay with me. . .please.' Suddenly she was shy. 'Maybe we should just go for that drink.'

'I have a bottle of champagne on ice in my car.' His eyes were warm with love. 'Will you share it with me?'

'Yes. . .please. And I do want to have more children, Marcus. Yours.'

PARTY TIME!

How would you like to win a year's supply of Mills & Boon® Books? Well, you can and they're FREE! Simply complete the competition below and send it to us by 31st August 1998. The first five correct entries picked after the closing date will each win a year's subscription to the Mills & Boon series of their choice. What could be easier?

BALLOONS	BUFFET	ENTERTAIN
STREAMER	DANCING	INVITE
DRINKS	CELEBRATE	FANCY DRESS
MUSIC	PARTIES	HANGOVER

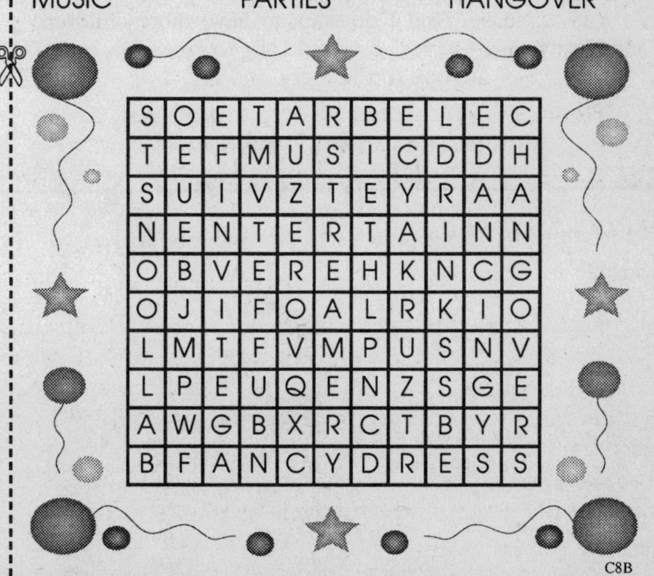

S	O	E	T	A	R	B	E	L	E	C
T	E	F	M	U	S	I	C	D	D	H
S	U	I	V	Z	T	E	Y	R	A	A
N	E	N	T	E	R	T	A	I	N	N
O	B	V	E	R	E	H	K	N	C	G
O	J	I	F	O	A	L	R	K	I	O
L	M	T	F	V	M	P	U	S	N	V
L	P	E	U	Q	E	N	Z	S	G	E
A	W	G	B	X	R	C	T	B	Y	R
B	F	A	N	C	Y	D	R	E	S	S

C8B

Please turn over for details of how to enter...

HOW TO ENTER

Can you find our twelve party words? They're all hidden somewhere in the grid. They can be read backwards, forwards, up, down or diagonally. As you find each word in the grid put a line through it. When you have completed your wordsearch, don't forget to fill in the coupon below, pop this page into an envelope and post it today—you don't even need a stamp!

Mills & Boon Party Time! Competition
FREEPOST CN81, Croydon, Surrey, CR9 3WZ
EIRE readers send competition to PO Box 4546, Dublin 24.

Please tick the series you would like to receive if you are one of the lucky winners

Presents™ ❑ Enchanted™ ❑ Medical Romance™ ❑
Historical Romance™ ❑ Temptation® ❑

Are you a Reader Service™ Subscriber? Yes ❑ No ❑

Mrs/Ms/Miss/Mr ....Intials ....
(BLOCK CAPITALS PLEASE)

Surname...

Address ....

....

....Postcode..........................

(I am over 18 years of age)

C8B

One application per household. Competition open to residents of the UK and Ireland only. You may be mailed with offers from other reputable companies as a result of this application. If you would prefer not to receive such offers, please tick box. ❑

Closing date for entries is 31st August 1998.